DEAD
MAN'S
GOLD

PICTURES BY

HARVEY CHAN

A GROUNDWOOD BOOK

DOUGLAS & McINTYRE

TORONTO VANCOUVER BERKELEY

PAUL YEE

DEAD MAN'S GOLD

AND OTHER STORIES

Groundwood Books / Douglas & McIntyre
720 Bathurst Street, Suite 500, Toronto, Ontario
Distributed in the USA by Publishers Group West
1700 Fourth Street, Berkeley, CA 94710

We acknowledge for their financial support of our publishing program the
Canada Council for the Arts, the Government of Canada through the Book
Publishing Industry Development Program (BPIDP), the Ontario Arts Council
and the Government of Ontario through the Ontario Media Development
Corporation's Ontario Book Initiative.

ONTARIO ARTS COUNCIL
CONSEIL DES ARTS DE L'ONTARIO

National Library of Canada Cataloguing in Publication Data
Yee, Paul
Dead man's gold and other stories
ISBN 0-88899-475-3 (bound). ISBN 0-88899-587-3 (pbk.)
1. Chinese--Canada--Juvenile literature. 2. Ghost stories, Canadian (English)
3. Children's stories, Canadian (English) I. Chan, Harvey II. Title.
PS8597.E3D42 2002   jC813'.54   C2002-901055-1
PZ7.J365De 2002

Library of Congress Control Number: 2002102190

Cover illustration by Harvey Chan
The illustrations for this book were done in Adobe Photoshop
Design by Michael Solomon
Printed and bound in Canada

To Troy and Cassandra Cardozo-Richardson,
from the past for the future

CONTENTS

ONE

DEAD MAN'S GOLD

◉

GOLD attracts men like a magnet awakening metal pins, like honey humming to bees. It shines and never rusts, flattens thin as tissue and reels into feathery threads. It crowns the kings of mighty empires and dazzles the eye when spun as filigree jewelry. It has caused nations to go to war, men to commit murder, and innocent people to be enslaved.

Chinese, too, have fallen under its strident glow and dark shadows.

In the mid-nineteenth century, when rumors of faraway gold rushes reached Big Field village in South China, many men decided to go to the New World, including Yuen and Fong. Born in the same month and same year, these two friends had chased tadpoles through ponds and played at the same school as children. Although both inherited plenty of farm chores, Yuen was the only son of poor peasants who owned a single pot to cook all their meals, while Fong's father had several fields, seven sons and two wives to manage his kitchen.

When it came time to leave, the families of both men gathered by the river to say farewell. Yuen's mother and sisters wept and clung to his sleeves, begging him not to go.

"I will send you news and gold as soon as I can," promised Yuen, but the women only wailed louder.

Fong stepped in. "Don't worry," he told them. "No matter where we go, we'll look after one another."

"Of course," added Yuen. "We'll stay together until we both get rich."

"Two heads are better than one," said Fong. "And four hands can carry any load."

So the women were comforted and the village men set forth.

In China, their black-brick village was snuggled in a coastal plain of rice paddies cultivated over many centuries. Ancient streams meandered by, and the horizon held low rolling hills. In the New World, the Big Field villagers shouldered picks and shovels and tramped through mountainous forests. They marveled at jagged, dark cliffs rising like castle walls, and at a river that boiled and churned through treacherous boulders.

Miners from around the world scrambled along the mighty river, its banks and many tributaries. Impatient to start, Fong often darted ahead to talk to miners who had already staked their claims on the river. He always returned in great excitement: "A man from Yen-ping was crossing a shallow stream when a glint in the water caught his eye. He crouched down and there lay a gold nugget round as a walnut, just waiting to be plucked!"

The villagers gathered as he continued, "Another man from our county took two fistfuls of gold gravel from nearby water. All in one day! A smart man, he stood at a bend in the river where the current slowed to drop its gold. He has returned to China to build two new houses!"

But the farther inland the villagers went, the costlier the supplies for daily living became. Soon the Big Field men faced a decision. Stop and take jobs working for other miners, or keep trekking until they could find an empty stretch of river where they could stake their own claims.

Yuen decided to hire himself out to miners, but Fong declared, "No one grows rich working for bosses. Don't stop here!"

"Poor families like mine have always relied on wages," Yuen insisted.

"Oh, just pull your belt tighter!" retorted his friend. "Come with me. Remember, we swore to stay together."

Yuen hung back. "Even if you go, you may never find gold. At least I will be paid."

"Paid?" Fong laughed. "You'll get pennies."

"Hah! You look down on hard work, yet you want instant riches."

"Of course I do. Don't you?"

As Fong stalked off, Yuen sighed and hoped his was the right decision.

"Hard work is heaven's way," he told himself. "That fool Fong has lived amidst abundance all his life. He has never ached or sweated from an honest day's toil."

Every day, Yuen hacked into the hard ground and dumped it into long sluices built from logs. There, river water roared through to wash away the dirt and leave behind the heavy gold. Yuen labored twelve back-breaking hours a day, for two dollars a shift. When rain or mosquitoes swarmed him, he wanted to run for shelter, but there was none nearby. What kept him working were thoughts of his mother and sisters, sniffling and waiting for news and money.

Just when he had saved enough to travel farther, the temperature dropped. All along the river, miners scurried south with packs on their backs and mules laden with equipment. They spoke of lakes freezing solid and thick, snowfalls higher than houses, and storms that devoured humans and horses.

The news alarmed him, so he wintered in the port city, too, and searched for Fong.

Other miners commented, "Your friend might have stayed north, or he might be dead and cold already." They invited him to games of dice and dominoes, but Yuen clung to his few pennies. Storekeepers who saw him frowned and looked away, for they knew at a glance that he had no money to spend.

Once winter retreated, he headed out again. The river ran high and fast with melting ice. Trekking north on muddy trails, he passed crude posts marking miners' claims, ragged tents and makeshift cabins, and graveyards guarding the unlucky.

Surely, he told himself, this time I will stake a claim on a section of this river.

But his savings were spent before he could reach an unoccupied stretch, so he found wage work standing in a shallow river. All day he shoveled mud and gravel into rocker boxes that strained the muck for gold. His legs turned numb and blue. At night he wrapped hot cloths around them, but they rarely warmed him. One day, he slipped and fell. His ankle swelled like an egg and ached, and by the time it healed, he had to head south for winter.

In the port city, Yuen ate low-grade rice and shared an attic with eight men. There was no room to stretch his legs, and he had no tales of lucky strikes to share. All winter he sat by the potbellied stove and stared glumly at the holes in his socks.

When spring returned, he headed north again. This time, with borrowed money, he purchased a second-hand claim — one given up as worthless by white miners. Chinese miners reworking such sites waded into the river to heave boulders and flushed out crevices with fine whisks. When they found gold, they crowed, "This is truly Gold Mountain."

Yuen found nothing — not a single nugget, not one speck of gold. He cursed heaven and earth, even damned his ancestors. Why did the precious metal of the New World evade him? But he kept on digging because images of his family tormented him. Night after night, he saw his parents huddled at a low bare table, holding empty bowls that gleamed in the dark.

One day, a familiar voice rang from the forest. There stood Fong in a leather jacket and gleaming boots that rose to his knees.

"What happened, old friend?" Fong shouted. "You're an ancient man of seventy!"

Yuen caught his reflection in the water. On a gaunt face, bloodshot eyes rolled in dark hollows and brown teeth hung loose. His skin had the color and texture of tree bark, while his hair bristled like a porcupine's.

He tried to smile. "And you, Fong, you haven't aged a day since we parted. You've done well?"

"Indeed!" He held up a weighty bag. In it Yuen saw the quiet gleam of gold nuggets, gold flakes and gold dust — enough for four lifetimes. He felt dizzy and clutched at his hat.

The two men strolled into the shade.

"Don't be envious," Fong said. "I wouldn't do this again, ever. I was frostbitten and huddled in a canvas tent under five blankets. Who knew the winter lasted six months! Then we starved because ice jammed the river and prevented supplies from reaching us. And I almost drowned when my horse and I rolled over a waterfall."

Yuen said nothing as he fingered the gold in the bag.

What an idiot I've been, he thought. If I had followed him, I would be a rich man, too! He wanted to pound his head hard against a tree. If he could have just half of Fong's gold, he could buy ten new paddy fields, rent them out, and build a spacious mansion for his family.

Fong added, "Bandits jumped my claim and tried to rob me, but I fought back with my rifle. Bears prowling for food wrecked my camp and sent me running up a tree. And like everyone else, I got sick and couldn't find a doctor. Sometimes I thought I would never see China again, or you, my friend."

Yuen nodded. "You are a lucky man. What next?"

Fong grinned. "I'm going home!"

When Yuen saw the gleaming white teeth in his friend's mouth, fury exploded inside him like overheated gunpowder. He slammed his shovel into Fong's head. His childhood friend fell to the ground, dead.

Yuen dropped the shovel and staggered back. What had he done?

But then China swirled through his mind. He imagined his scrawny ragged parents kneeling in the market square, weakly begging for food. Fong's family would be healthy, crowded around a table crammed with fish and chicken, vegetables and eggs. They even had enough to feed the stray dogs of the village.

In the woods, Yuen removed his friend's clothing and boots, buried them, and left the body for hungry wolves. No one would ever trace Fong's last steps. In a frontier so vast and deep, who would notice that one Chinese miner had gone missing?

In the port city, Yuen visited steam baths and scrubbed himself with stiff brushes. At the tailor, he ordered new suits and shirts. When his ship set sail for China, he felt as fresh and clean as a newborn babe, and he vowed never to return. In bustling Hong Kong, he bought extravagant gifts before heading home.

At Big Field village, the neighbors attended Yuen's banquet. Enviously, they watched him present a watch chain to his father, earrings to his mother, and necklaces to his sisters, all fashioned from pure gold. Plans for a new house were announced and everyone congratulated the successful miner.

When Fong's mother came up, Yuen saw that her hair had whitened, and her back was bowed over.

"Do you have news of my son?" she asked.

Yuen pressed two gold coins into her hand and turned away, but she cried out, "You two vowed to get rich side by side, or to return home in disgrace together! What happened? Tell me!"

She thrust forth her wrinkled face, but he could not

bear to look her in the eyes. Panicked, he pushed her aside and hurried off.

Then, within a week of Yuen's return, his mother donned her new earrings and went to wash in the creek. Days later, an ear infection rendered her deaf. The watch chain hung from the father's vest during his walk over the dikes. He fell and became paralyzed. At her home, Yuen's older sister was dangling her necklace at her child when he suddenly tipped onto the stone floor. After that, the child never spoke or cried again.

The villagers averted their eyes and whispered about cursed gold. When they persisted in asking about Fong, Yuen replied, "Gold Mountain is wild and dangerous. Animals might have devoured him, the river could have carried him off, or an avalanche may have suffocated him."

"Alas, Heaven can be cruel," cried the villagers. "Hopefully, his body has been properly buried. Without a safe home so far away, his soul will never rest."

Yuen swallowed hard and tears slipped from his eyes.

Then his younger sister rushed in and flung her necklace at him. Weeping, she shouted, "This carries nothing but bad luck!"

After that, Yuen announced he would return to Gold Mountain to search for his friend.

During the ocean voyage, he braced himself on the tilting deck as waves battered the sailing ship. If only he could restore the heartbeat in Fong, send warm blood coursing through a dead man's veins. He needed to loosen the curse on his family and prepare an offering worthy of his friend.

After much thought, he started whittling on a piece of wood.

In the port city, he visited a jeweler and threw all the gold items his family had worn into a blazing furnace. Afterwards, he ordered the lump of gold smashed and pounded and ground into fine powder. Then he trekked north.

For weeks he pushed through the bush toward the source of the great river that had carried gold throughout the land. He crashed through thick undergrowth and clambered over decaying logs. Blackflies tormented him until he bled. Rain fell steadily. Onward he pressed, climbing to heights slippery and cold.

Finally he reached the mountaintop where the river started. He opened the sack of gold dust and sprinkled it over the stream.

He watched the current eddy away and silently prayed:

"All you who find this dust must honor Fong.
He found the gold, but passed it along."

Then, after days of walking back, he reached the site of his old claim. It was deserted, for no one expected to find gold there. In the silent forest nearby, he dug for Fong's clothing and spent the day deepening the hole, one shovelful after another. The soil went into huge canvas bags that were rolled over the narrow grave. At its head, he planted a wooden marker carved with Fong's name, dates and home village, along with sticks of sweet incense and long candles. Then he pulled on his friend's dank clothing and slid under the canvas bags into the pit. Stretching out his legs, he breathed deeply and shut his eyes. Then he jabbed a sharp knife upwards and slashed the bags. Dirt gushed out and smothered him.

By making his body the bed for his friend's soul, Yuen broke the deadly curse. Back in the village, his father staggered out of bed to hobble through the laneways, and his mother's hearing gradually returned, just in time to hear her grandson coo and laugh like any other toddler.

But Yuen's own restless spirit was left without a natural home. Ever since that day, miners passing through gold territory often saw a pale, sad face peering out from near the river.

TWO
DIGGING DEEP

⊙

WHEN Chung was born, his parents exploded long strings of red firecrackers to celebrate, having waited many years for his birth. Because he was an only child, his mother fussed endlessly. She laced shoes on him when all the other boys ran barefoot, halted rough playing in the cobblestone lanes, and forbade him to approach the peddlers traveling from town to town with trinkets and toys.

Chung grew up fearful of strangers, surprises and the smallest pain. He was even afraid of the dark. After sunset, he crawled into bed and avoided the outhouse until morning. He slept close to the window, always hoping for moonlight to shine through. If the family chickens squawked at a fox in the middle of the night, his mother had to run out and drive it off. On returning, she poked her son and grumbled, "When will you go and do this job?"

Chung wasn't proud of himself, but fear clung like a shadow no matter how hard he tried to shake it loose.

When Chung turned seventeen, the mother said, "Son, you must marry soon. Nothing would make your father and me happier than grandchildren playing at our feet and a daughter-in-law caring for us. You know Chinese tradition dictates this."

Chung turned pale. He knew any wife would scorn a husband who feared the dark.

"Who will marry a man so poor?" he blustered. "And how would we feed more mouths?" Then he gave an answer he hoped would free him. "I will go abroad and work. In Gold Mountain, riches shimmer in the rivers, waiting like wildflowers to be picked. I can bring back enough gold to support you and a wife and many grandchildren."

His mother was the only village matron without gold earrings, and soon she convinced herself the New World did offer fine opportunities for her son. There he would overcome his childhood fears and become a man every villager would respect.

Chung reached the New World and saw Chinese waiting at the docks with cloth-tied bundles. When he asked directions to the newest gold fields, the men laughed.

"Young fellow, haven't you heard? The gold rush is finished! All the gold is gone, shipped to bank vaults in big cities. All you'll find here is gray rock and wild animals. You'd better head home with us."

But Chung couldn't. His parents had borrowed large sums to buy his passage. They expected good news. If he returned empty-handed, the villagers would label him a failure and a greater coward than ever.

He found his way to Chinatown, to a store that rented plank-board beds to travelers.

"Uncle," he said, "is it true there is no gold left?"

The storekeeper nodded grimly, but Chung insisted, "There must be work here."

"A little. Were you a farmer's son?"

He nodded.

"Then there is nothing for you."

The young man bristled. "Why do you say that?"

"You lived on a farm where sunshine warmed your back, did you not? You stood tall and gazed across green and golden fields, did you not?"

"I did."

"Well, this job lies deep underground, with foul air and no light. Human skin turns pale and black at the same time. Every month, sometimes every week, a man is killed. The work is very dangerous."

Chung quelled his panic and stammered, "I'm not afraid."

A slow ferry chugged up the island, and a train carried him to the mine. Through the trees he saw flashes of sparkling inland water. Then he heard the jangle of bells, tinny but urgent as a temple on fire. Chung's heart began to pound.

He stumbled off the train into the stench of rotting eggs. When his eyes stopped watering, he saw the ground crisscrossed by railway tracks running helter-skelter — into a yawning cave, into sheds with long rolling tables, and down toward a harbor. Ornery locomotives rumbled by, dragging carts of shiny black rock. Their heavy wheels bit into steel and screeched until loads were dumped with a deafening roar. Chimneys poked from brick buildings and spewed storm clouds of steam and smoke. From the looming darkness of the mine echoed a metallic thunder —

clank, clank, clank, clank — as if a monstrous heart throbbed deep down there.

That night, Chung did not sleep. The hissing steam and cranking machines went on without stop. His hands grew cold and stiff as the hour for going underground drew near.

In the morning, he went to the cage that dropped into the mine, but he trembled so badly that his hammer and hand-drill rattled like a teacup and saucer. When the miners hooted, Chung grit his teeth and said to himself, "I would give anything to be brave!"

He gripped the iron bars as pulleys squealed like pigs being slaughtered. During the descent, the air cooled and dampened and turned sour. Above him, the shaft entrance shrank to a pinprick, and the men's faces turned gray, then black before vanishing altogether. A familiar fear gripped his body. No one heard him mutter, "I would give anything not to be frightened!"

Finally, the cage stopped and the men were sent into a maze of low tunnels. Chung donned a lamp-hat reeking of fish oil. He crawled through mud, under wooden beams and past carts dragged by weary mules. His fingers groped for the miners ahead.

I have arrived in hell, he thought. Hundreds of ghosts must hover here at their death sites. Again he muttered, "I would give anything to have courage!"

The coal seam sank deep into the ground, so the miners lay on their bellies and aimed their tools by touch. At the slightest creak, Chung froze, expecting the roof to collapse, expecting to be buried alive. But nearby miners calmly continued working. He wanted to scream, to break free and out of the belly of this beast.

That night, an exhausted Chung dreamed of the cage dropping into the mine. But this time, he didn't tremble or clutch at the bars. To his surprise, he threw out his chest and sucked in gulps of air like the winner of a long race.

A miner with a bushy mustache clapped his shoulder.

"Do I know you?" Chung asked.

The other man smiled. "Friend, you called for me today. Earlier, you offered to give anything for courage. So I am removing your fear."

"But who are you?" Chung asked.

"Me? I am all the miners who have died here. I am their courage and humor, the spirit that defied all danger and all greedy bosses."

"Do you help all miners?"

"No." He laughed bitterly. "They find my price too high."

"What do you charge?"

"I require your body to replace mine, which is rotting away under a fallen tunnel. I need a strong new resting place for my soul and all the memories I carry. Is this agreeable to you?"

"How long do I have?"

"Until you take a bride."

Chung thought for a moment. If he didn't steel himself to earn some money here, he would never get a bride anyway. So he shouted, "Agreed!"

After that, Chung marched eagerly to work each day. He never floundered or lost his way underground. He tracked seams of coal deep into the earth and sniffed for rock gas that could easily explode. Each day, he ripped out cartfuls of coal and sent them up as roving packs of rats nudged his tools and meal bucket.

In the meantime, Chung sent his wages home. After each remittance, a letter would arrive from his parents, saying they were proud and the other villagers were jealous. For the first time in his life, Chung walked with his head held high.

He also acquired a reputation for being lucky. When water flooded a tunnel and drowned two miners, Chung escaped through an adjacent passage. When a roof collapsed and crushed several men, a beam fell over Chung and saved him. When a laden cart suddenly broke loose and hurtled toward his group, only Chung squeezed out of the way. Soon all the miners clamored to work near him, thinking the gods had blessed him. But he knew the mustached spirit was protecting him only to ensure his body would remain intact and healthy.

In the bunkhouse, the miners played cards and gambled between shifts. One night, after a late session of dominoes, Chung dozed and dreamed of the miner with the bushy mustache.

"Young man, you've done well all these years," the ghost said. "Haven't you saved enough money for a fancy wedding? Isn't it time to do your family duty?"

"No!" Chung bolted upright. He looked around the crowded bunkhouse and heard the sounds of men sleeping.

These are my friends, he thought. They trust me and follow me through the tunnels. In this country, I am a man among men.

Later that day, he received a letter from his mother: "Son, you have sent us much money and we are very grateful. Now send yourself home to get married."

Chung dispatched a letter saying he could not abandon his workmates.

Months later, his mother sent word and ordered his return. "The longer you wait," she stated, "the less choice of brides you will have."

He crumpled the letter and threw it away.

That very night, the miner with the bushy mustache interrupted his dreams and said, "Listen to your mother. It is time to get married. You cannot defy your destiny, nor can you escape our agreement."

Chung groaned loudly, and his bunkmates woke him to break the nightmare.

His mother's words grew sterner. "You are our only child," said one letter. "We raised you with love and attention. All we ask in return is respect for tradition. Can we depend on you to do the right thing?"

Another letter wailed, "Your father lies in bed all day, too ashamed to meet his friends. Those men carry their grandchildren through the village, swinging them along and singing. They sit by the fishpond under the banyan tree. How can you neglect your father thus?"

One day, thunder tore through the underground tunnels. Chung heard timber cracking, men screaming for help and the braying of panicked mules. Far above, a shrill whistle summoned help. Grit rained down and extinguished his lantern. He ran toward the exit, but it was blocked. His bare hands tugged at rock, but the slabs weighed too much.

Trapped, he dropped to the ground. As usual, he felt no fear, confident that his guardian spirit would protect him. Nor did he smell the after-damp, the odorless, poisonous gas released by explosions. His eyelids felt heavy and soon they fell shut forever.

Days later, when the mine bosses announced that they were stopping the search for Chung's body, the other miners shook their heads and sighed, "Nobody's luck can last forever."

A few days later, another letter came for Chung. His friends opened it and read, "Son, we could wait no longer. Since you refuse to return, we have selected a bride for you and conducted a marriage ceremony. Your new wife is now living in our house, sleeping in your bed and eagerly awaiting you. When you come home, she will greet you with respect."

THREE

SKY-HIGH

◉

IN the southern city of Canton, any guest to Shu's home would have instantly seen how rich this family was, for its front courtyard contained a grove of trees, none of which bore fruit. Shu's ancestors had planted them for their natural beauty — the rugged bends of sturdy trunks, the elegant silhouette of high-reaching branches — unlike practical folk who cultivated trees for edible fruit. On nights of the full moon, the entire family stood outside and admired the silvery disk floating over the leafy skyline. In the summer, servants faithfully watered the roots, and in the fall, they cleared leaves from beneath the twists of drying branches.

As youngest son, Shu enjoyed a long childhood. Eldest Brother followed Father in the family business, Second Brother studied for the Imperial exams, and Third Brother attended the military academy. But Shu strolled among the trees, read poetry in their shade and climbed them to hide from the servants. The family took care of all his needs, and his time was spent with friends at teahouses, hillside villas and calligraphy contests.

Then Father died suddenly. The family conducted a

stately funeral attended by high officials and powerful merchants. Shu performed the rites solemnly, for he had respected his father.

Then, after the rituals were finished, the family discovered Father had concealed enormous debts in every city and country he had visited. When the banks, money-lenders and gambling-hall operators clamored in the courts for repayment, the family was forced to sell everything: the business and its warehouses, the mansion and its trees, all the fine furniture and everybody's personal belongings.

The brothers took jobs to feed their wives and children, but Shu had no skills. He avoided his friends who sneered at his bad luck. He wanted to leave town, but his father's reputation stretched far and wide, inside China and out.

One of the few places where his family hadn't done business was Gold Mountain, and that become Shu's destination. Off he sailed, with only the clothes on his back and a book of poems rescued from the family library.

In Chinatown, the job boss declared, "All I have are logging jobs."

He outfitted Shu in flannel shirt, stiff denim pants and caulk boots, but the new clothes could not make him stronger or bigger. Skinny and pale, Shu wriggled like a worm emerging from mucky soil. At the docks he met the crew. They saw by his words and his walk that he had fallen from an upper class. His smooth skin revealed he had never worked or suffered.

They sailed up the coast through a gray mist as rough waves pummeled the company boat. Craggy cliffs covered with forests rose into view. The boat came to a deep bay where trees marched to the waterline. Each one was so tall and thick that ten men with arms linked could barely circle its trunk. The trees were straight as pillars at a grand temple, with the sky above forming its roof.

Never before had Shu seen such proud growth. China had razed its forests for farms and cities long ago, and the trees at his family home were puny saplings in comparison.

Moved by this grandeur, he recited two lines of poetry:

"Trees along heaven's edge grow neat as grass
And land gleams moon-like while waters pass."

The crew chortled and tossed him into the saltwater like a sack of garbage. Shu sputtered and flailed helplessly, for he couldn't swim. The men chuckled as he bobbed up and down.

"Let's see if rich boys sink as fast as poor ones," they said.

Finally the cook threw out a rope and Shu grabbed it.

In the forest, he wielded a long ax while balanced on a springboard jammed into the tree's trunk. He splashed kerosene onto long saws to make them slide through the unyielding wood. When a tree fell, he hacked off branches and sawed them into sections. A single tree created four or more days of work before its logs hit the water to be towed to a mill.

The Pacific Northwest was cold and wet. Dark clouds pushed in from the sea and rain fell for days, even weeks. Shu struggled to walk in cracked and leaky boots as sheets of water washed his face and stung his eyes. When the rain stopped, the puddles bred mosquitoes — thousands and thousands of buzzing pests, all thirsty for human blood.

Desperately, he rubbed grease and wax and soot onto his skin to thwart them, but the insects sneaked into the tents, drawn by lamplight and the smell of wet socks.

Thick calluses erupted on Shu's hands, and his skin grew red and hard from bites. His body ached as muscles filled his arms and shoulders. At night, he took a lantern and tramped into the woods to read aloud, letting the rhymes and images of poetry relax him.

The men heard him reading alone and imitated him, but chanted jumpy rhythms to spoil the lines. At mealtimes, they mimicked how he held his rice bowl, used his chopsticks and pulled fish bones from his teeth instead of spitting them out.

Shu saw their mocking faces but his ears focused elsewhere: the tide washing over shoreline sand, the fluttering of birds' wings at treetops, or the toot of a ship passing far out at sea.

Meanwhile, the loggers pushed inland, and the greased path that took the logs to the water grew longer.

One day, as Shu swung his ax into a tree, he heard strange sounds. It wasn't the seagulls cawing and gliding overhead or the distant grunts of grizzly bears. The sounds were deep groans, long sighs and sharp yelps of pain. They came loudest after each thwack of the ax. Both human and animal at once, the sounds chilled Shu to the bone.

Across from him, his partner showed no signs of distress, so Shu kept quiet. All day long, he chopped and sawed. The sounds grew louder, as if the entire forest were moaning and suffering. But the crew worked on, as if deaf.

That night in camp, Shu hardly tasted his rice and fish. After tea, he grabbed his book and lantern and went into the forest. The round faces of stumps caught the moon's light as tree sap oozed out and dripped down the bark like teardrops. All he heard was the swish of waves from the beach.

From his book, he read aloud:

"Along seven clear strings,
Silent pines are sliced by winds
With old songs long adored
That no one performs any more."

When he had finished, the leaves above him swayed and rustled, even though the night air hung heavy and still. He trudged deeper into the woods, to the biggest tree there. He had named it Sky-High. Its trunk was twice as thick as the largest tree he had felled. Shu had counted the rings on that stump, and now calculated that Sky-High was at least two thousand years old. Fellow trees guarded it closely, so he couldn't see through to the top. In the presence of this grand and natural tower, he felt enormous peace, as if he were at home reading in the family mansion.

Back at camp, the men were snoring, but the cook was waiting. He bent close and whispered, "Did you hear sounds in the forest today?"

Shu nodded. "What was it?"

The cook looked around to make sure no one was listening.

"After my first season in the bush," he said, "a wise man told me it was the forest weeping."

"Like the sap running out of the stumps!" exclaimed Shu.

"Trees are living things, and the more we chop, the

greater the pain of the forest. I used to be a logger but I quit. That's why I cook now."

"I'll do the same," declared Shu, but the older man shook his head.

"Won't matter," he said grimly. "The company will hire someone else. There's easy money here, so trees will keep falling."

"We're killers!"

"No, we're men with families to feed."

That night, Shu couldn't sleep with the sounds of the forest's moaning. He knew it was only a matter of time before the loggers reached his friend Sky-High and chopped it down.

That must not happen, he thought.

Then came a big holiday, and the company boat took the men to town. Shu offered to stay behind to guard the supplies.

Once the boat had sailed out of sight, he dragged the axes and saws to deep water and let them sink. With several trips, he emptied the camp of all its sharpened steel. Then he punctured all the freshwater barrels and let the drinking water trickle away.

Shu packed some food, planning to trek down the coast. Before leaving, he visited Sky-High one last time.

He looked up at the perfect lines of the tree. He breathed in the aromatic sweetness and wished he could catch the view from its top.

When the loggers returned and discovered the destruction, they stomped through the forest, vowing to beat Shu senseless. The company boat took men and torches to search the coastline.

They discovered his crumpled body at the foot of the giant tree, and thought he had fallen while climbing to hide from them. The men cursed and hurled dishes around, but nothing could be done. Soon the company boat ferried them away.

A year later, a new crew arrived at the site and tried to chop down Sky-High. But the loggers ran away, badly frightened. At first, these men refused to discuss what had happened, but slowly a strange story emerged.

When tools were put down, they vanished into thin air. The loggers thought animals were dragging them off but no tracks were left on the soft ground. Often an unknown voice whispered and chuckled around the men, as if laughing at them. And the air around Sky-High's trunk stayed icy cold throughout the day, even when sunlight hit the ground.

Finally, when the loggers raised their axes, a Chinese man with a pale face appeared before them. When they tried to shove him aside, their thick hands passed right through his body.

* * *

To this day, the towering tree called Sky-High still stands. The wind rustles through its branches, and lines heard long ago drift to the ground:

"On northern mountains amidst white clouds,
Hermits come to seek their peace.
Climbing high to avoid all crowds,
Where hearts can soar with wild geese.
Sadness rises from a quiet dusk,
As autumn air turns clear and brisk."

FOUR

THE MEMORY STONE

◉

TO Chinese people, jade is the most magical of stones. When adorning human skin, it absorbs the body's oils and essences as well as the owner's nature, whether the person is soft or hard, warm or cold. Its healing touch can cool a fever or calm a chill. It can also be ground into powder and swallowed as a tonic.

The Chinatown museum owns a jade pendant, centuries old, the shape and size of a large coin. Cloudy green in color, its surface is as clear and smooth as water, but one side has a hairline crack running from its edge to center. For collectors, however, this feature only increases the value.

Many stories accompany this stone, but the best known comes from the turn of the century and starts in South China's Pearl River region.

* * *

Willow, a young widow, lived in a busy town where three rivers became one on their way to the ocean. Many boats passed by, so Willow and her mother-in-law opened a guesthouse that provided clean beds and hearty meals. Many men requested Willow's hand in remarriage, but she remained devoted to the memory of her husband, a kind and gentle man.

Early one morning, a beggar pounded on the back door.

"Show some heart," he shouted. "I'm going to Gold Mountain to get rich. You'll soon be rewarded!"

Willow opened the door and her mouth dropped open. She saw a face almost identical to her husband's. Her late spouse's piercing eyes and toothy smile had stayed fresh in her memory for a long time, and she never imagined seeing them again. Her hand almost reached out to touch the stranger's face.

"Work for me," she said, "and I will pay you the going wage. You'll sleep in the stable and eat rice twice a day."

He called himself Ox, from the hill country. A blacksmith who planned to work with horses, he loved all animals. He fed exhausted packhorses slowly, to prevent stomach pains. He changed the straw in the stables every day and scrubbed the mules clean. When he whistled, wild dogs came running; when he clucked his tongue, chickens flocked at his feet. When he filled the feeding trough in the pigpen, one little piglet always nibbled at his trouser. In the fall, when the fattened hog was dispatched to the butcher, Willow saw Ox's lips tremble, and at that moment, she lost her heart to him.

At his departure, he said, "Wait for me, Willow, and I will return to wed you."

"Many men want me and my guesthouse," she said. "Why should I wait?"

"Because my feelings for you are the truest and the strongest." From behind his back he brought out a small bamboo cage. "This little canary will sing to our love every day."

Willow was startled. She had never owned a songbird, but the yellow-green creature had a clean sweet voice that instantly soothed her.

She fumbled for a return gift. Her apron pockets were empty, so from her neck she unfastened a jade pendant.

"Take this," she said, "and I will wait for you. This stone has been handed down by men and women in my family over many generations. My father claims it guards my well-being, so if you change your mind about me, you must return it."

Ox bent close and whispered, "You can trust me."

Willow kept the birdcage by her bed and listened to the trilling early in the morning and late at night. Every day, she fed the bird grains and greens.

After many months, she released the bird from its cage to see what would happen. It fluttered to the ceiling and to the four corners of the room. It danced atop the cabinet and flew by the open window and the door. But it remained inside and always landed on Willow's shoulder and hands. She stroked the tiny head and wings, and delighted at its soft feathers and gentle warmth.

She sent letters to Ox, but he replied infrequently, complaining about how hard it was to find work.

Then she awoke one day and found the cage empty and the bird gone. For days she searched the nearby forest and streets and waited fretfully, but the canary did not return. Her heart clenched like a fighter's fist, and she could neither eat nor talk. For weeks she waited in vain for Ox's letters, but they had stopped coming.

Her mother-in-law said, "Didn't I warn you about Gold Mountain men? They leave you, and great distances cloud their memories. That man will never keep his promise. You should forget about him."

Instead, Willow decided to travel to the New World. For the first time in her life, she journeyed down the river she saw daily. At the great ocean port of Hong Kong, frantic crowds pushed at her from all sides — on the docks, in the narrow streets, and even in the guarded lobby of her hotel. Never before had she seen so many people. Her room was tiny and dank, and she gladly boarded the steamship at sailing time. Traveling alone, she took a second-class cabin for privacy and safety.

For days all Willow saw were blue skies and a blue ocean. Seagulls with broad wingspans hovered close, cawing and dipping by her porthole, but soon they veered away. In her cabin, she tried on the Western hats and dresses she had purchased in Hong Kong. Ox had lived in the New World for so long that she thought he would probably prefer to see her dressed like a modern woman.

When the boat docked, Willow's legs and feet felt weak and unsteady as she laced her boots. She stumbled down the gangplank, heavy bags banging at her knees, only to end up spending hours with immigration officials and translators. She pleaded she was just a visitor and not a settler who should pay the head tax, a fee that only Chinese immigrants paid to settle in the country.

"I came to visit a friend."

"I have a thriving business in China. Why would I abandon it?"

"My family is in China. Of course I want to go back."

DEAD MAN'S GOLD

When they finally released her, she headed to Chinatown in a horse-drawn buggy. The roads were jammed with wagons and horses, great metal boxes grunting on steel tracks, and small carts with black rubber wheels that ran on their own power. In Chinatown, she recognized people who had passed through her inn long ago. Some had become plump and others thin, while some had grown mustaches. But nobody recalled her face, everyone wore Western clothes, and some even spoke English.

She stopped at a guesthouse to store her bags and comb her hair. In the mirror over the washstand, she saw deep lines around her eyes and wondered if Ox would notice.

Downstairs, she stopped at the front door to get her bearings. A shrill blast from the train station across the way startled her, and then the ferocious squeal of moving iron machinery filled the air. She clutched her hat and took a step back.

"How will I ever find Ox in such a noisy, crowded city?" she asked herself.

At that very moment, Ox strode by, looking healthy and contented in a Western suit and polished boots. A woman's delicate hand was tucked into the crook of his arm. She was as plain as a doorknob, but Ox's face glowed with pleasure.

The sighting plunged a blunt knife into Willow's heart as years of love seeped away.

She retreated into the hotel and gasped, "Who is that?"

"Why, that is Ox Woo and his new bride! Her father is a gambler who made a fortune at the racetracks. Those two were married six weeks ago." The chatty innkeeper added, "Some people say she looks like a horse, too, but she does own a dozen racing steeds. She met her husband-to-be in the stables, where he was a hired hand cleaning the stalls."

Willow turned and dashed up the stairs. She repacked her bags and returned to the ship terminal. She vowed to never love another man, even if that meant never bearing children. At home, she flung Ox's bamboo birdcage into the stove, where it burst into crackling flames.

At this time, Ox noticed that a crack had suddenly appeared on one side of his jade pendant.

"What does this mean?" he roared, and his wife came running.

She looked closely and said, "Send it back to Willow. It is not yours to keep."

"Nonsense," he declared. "This marvelous stone belongs to our firstborn child."

"No," she cried, "it will bring bad luck."

But Ox would not listen.

Soon, a daughter was born to them, named Blossom. Her features were very pleasing to the eye, and Ox gave her the jade pendant, which she wore all the time.

One day, when Blossom was five years old, Ox saddled up his favorite horse and took her riding. On the wooded trail, a bird suddenly darted from the bushes and spooked the horse. It reared up and threw off its riders. Ox hit his head on a sharp rock and died instantly, while Blossom became tangled in the reins and was dragged over the trail. She spent several months in a hospital, and when the doctors removed the bandages, a scar zigzagged across half her face. Her mother almost fainted, for its shape was identical to the crack on the jade. The doctors said nothing could be done, for the wound was deep. In her grief, Blossom's mother took the jade pendant and hurled it into the ocean.

Under her mother's care, Blossom grew into a good-natured girl with many friends. Like her father, she was devoted to animals. She brought home birds with broken wings and tried to nurse them back to health. Stray dogs followed her, and she begged to keep them. When the neighbor's cat had a litter of kittens, she pleaded for one. At school, she wrote stories about insects and whales.

But her mother fretted about the scar, worrying that no man would marry her. She took Blossom to doctors and surgeons all over North America, but they all agreed the damage was permanent.

When Blossom turned seventeen, the mother asked, "What do you want for your birthday dinner?"

"Bean-cake!"

"But that is so ordinary. How about roast chicken or barbecued duck?"

Blossom made a face. "You know I don't like eating meat."

The mother decided to stuff the soft bean-cake with fish-paste, so she sent the cook to the market to buy a fresh fish. She planned other dishes of eggs, nuts and vegetables and invited all of Blossom's friends.

Then the cook came running from the kitchen, his hands wet and glistening. "Look what I found in the fish's stomach!"

He held up the jade pendant that had been thrown into the ocean years ago. The mother recognized the jagged shape of the crack right away.

Late that night, she sat down with Blossom. "There is something in our possession that must be returned to its rightful owner. Are you ready for a trip to China?"

So Blossom boarded a steamship and journeyed to the town where three rivers met. She passed village after village with ancient houses of blackened brick and green-tiled roofs. Barefoot children on the riverbank waved at her.

Blossom had never set foot in China before, yet somehow the bend of the river, the leafy spread of the chestnut tree, the curve of the stone bridge all seemed familiar.

Finally she reached the guesthouse where her father had worked two decades earlier, and she asked for Willow.

At the door, the mother-in-law gasped and fell against the frame. Blossom thought perhaps she had never seen a woman from Gold Mountain, and certainly not one with such a vivid scar.

She held out a silk pouch containing the jade.

"This belongs to Willow."

The mother-in-law beckoned her to follow.

In her room, Willow knelt on the floor with her back straight and eyes closed, in front of an altar laden with flowers and fruit. The mother-in-law whispered to Blossom, "She finds peace in praying each day." Then she went and slid the jade pendant into Willow's calm hands.

Willow's eyes flew open. "Who brought this?"

Blossom stepped forward. "I did."

Willow spun around and the eyes of the two women sprang wide with amazement. Aside from the scar, Blossom looked exactly like the Willow of twenty years before. Their tapered chins, the full cheeks and the tiny mouths were identical.

Willow gripped her jade pendant tightly. The years of anger melted as she stroked Blossom's face.

"Here," Willow said, handing her the pendant. "Rub this jade over your scar every day. You, your mother and I, we have all suffered enough."

When Blossom took the jade, she was astounded to feel its warmth. The stone seemed to glow with new luster. Holding it to her face, she felt her cheek tingle.

Gradually her scar dissolved and she returned to the New World with Willow's blessings. In time, she married and gave birth to many children.

As for Willow, she worked contentedly at her guesthouse for the rest of her life, knowing she had a daughter in Blossom. And it was one of Blossom's grandchildren, a woman named Jade, who donated the pendant to the Chinatown museum. It sits in a glass case by a window, where visitors marvel at how natural light changes the look of the stone from hour to hour.

Blossom's granddaughter left special instructions for the care of the pendant. Once a month, the stone is removed from the glass case. Under the watchful eyes of security guards, it is passed by hand from one visitor to another.

And as they grip it in their palms or press it to their cheeks, smiles fill their faces.

FIVE

SEAWALL SIGHTINGS

⊙

I N 1975, citizens hardly noticed when bulldozers demolished the Immigration Building, known to the old-timer Chinese as Pig Pen. Its barred windows and high walls occupied downtown land adjacent to a seaside park, the harbor and railway lines. Over the years, thousands of Chinese immigrants had landed and undergone humiliating inspections there, until the gateway for newcomers shifted to the airport.

One foggy evening, shortly after the fall of Pig Pen, a cyclist raced along the nearby seawall, dodging puddles left by heavy rains. He leaned into a curve and inadvertently churned up a spray of water that drenched two Chinese pedestrians. He wheeled around to apologize, but to his surprise, nobody was there. He rode for a distance in both directions but didn't spot a soul. They couldn't have clambered up the muddy cliffs because of their formal dress — she in a long dress, he in a dark suit and polished shoes.

On another day, a retired businessman took a late afternoon stroll after a fierce windstorm. A loosened shoelace stopped him at a park bench, where he watched two young Chinese stroll by arm in arm — she in an evening gown and he in a formal tuxedo. The businessman preferred solitary walks, so he let them swing around the bend before following. On reaching the same corner, he saw a huge tree blocking the way. It had crashed down during the storm. On one side of the path rose a steep cliff; on the other was deep water. But the young couple had vanished.

Months later, the businessman's granddaughter went to the federal archives in the nation's capital to research the family's history. She spent weeks searching through boxes of records from the Department of Immigration. One afternoon, she flipped open a thick file marked "Yung, Gim-lan — Attempted Illegal Entry." Little did she know that this folder, yellowed and flaking after fifty years, contained the clues to her grandfather's sighting that afternoon.

* * *

Choi Jee-yun was the only daughter of a wealthy merchant in Hong Kong. Although he had wanted a son, in 1912 China it was considered progressive to treat girls equal to boys. It was also viewed as modern to adopt Western ideas, so when she grew older, he let her ride an imported bicycle at home and attend a missionary school for girls. Jee-yun treasured going to classes, for her girl cousins were not allowed to attend school and never left the family compound.

Jee-yun scored high marks and the teachers encouraged her to advance to college for more education. Her father worried about the male students in those classes, but his reputation as a forward-thinking businessman was at stake, so he let her enroll. Secretly, he instructed a servant to watch her every move.

The servant brought back disturbing news. A young man named Yen Wah-lung was regularly walking Jee-yun home. When she stayed late at school, Wah-lung also remained behind. The two studied the same subjects, did homework together and attended concerts with other friends.

Jee-yun's father withdrew his daughter from school, claiming a private tutor at home would benefit her more. He advised her not to attend concerts at night because the streets had become lawless and dangerous. The household servants were ordered not to admit male visitors and to inspect all packages addressed to her.

Of course Jee-yun and Wah-lung knew of her father's opposition. Wah-lung's father operated a candle stall in the old market and possessed limited education, while Jee-yun's father befriended international bankers to expand his business empire. A cousin agreed to carry secret messages between the young lovers, and after months of painful separation, they decided to flee to the New World. Wah-lung would leave first, find a job and lay the foundations for a life together.

"I will set up an apartment for us," he promised in his last letter before leaving. "It will have tall windows to let in sunlight, and all the furnishings will be of the highest quality. As soon as you join me, I will put on a new suit and you will slip into a long elegant gown and we will attend a symphony concert together."

When Jee-yun's father heard of Wah-lung's departure, he smiled to himself. Meanwhile, Jee-yun purchased stacks of books and piled them high on her desk and shelves to give the impression that she was trying to forget about her young man by immersing herself in her studies.

When Wah-lung's boat sailed into the New World harbor, the mountains and water reminded him of home and left him longing for Jee-yun. He marveled at wide roads filled with gleaming automobiles and at green lawns surrounding lofty houses. His sweetheart would be very happy here, he thought. But he also noticed the Chinese lived in the poorer section of town and labored at low-paying jobs.

The only work he could find was clerking in a downtown store selling silks and curios from China and Japan. To save money, he walked an hour to work instead of riding the streetcar. When he shopped for food, he selected limp greens being sold at half price. The room he found for himself was dim and tiny. When people invited him to a teahouse or game-hall, he always said no. And he resisted the temptation to buy newspapers, even though Chinatown published five papers, which citizens devoured for news of local and worldwide events.

But skimping on newspapers and teahouse gossip proved costly. Wah-lung came home one day to discover the government had slammed the door on his beloved Jee-yun's entry. Chinese migrants had kept arriving despite a head tax, and now the government decided to keep the nation white by banning their immigration altogether.

Right away, he sent a telegram to Hong Kong, advising Jee-yun to stay calm and promising a new plan to reunite them. She wrote back saying she trusted him with all her heart.

A year later, he used all his savings to buy the birth certificate of a Chinese born in North America. He sent it to Jee-yun, who told her father she was going on a shopping trip to Japan. She journeyed across the Pacific as Yung Gim-lan, a citizen of the New World who had been sent to her father's village at an early age and was now returning to her country of birth.

But when Jee-yun's ship docked, she was escorted into Pig Pen and told that her documents would be examined there. Guards marched her to a room containing only a table, with four chairs behind it and one in front. Iron bars guarded the windows.

Three officials and an interpreter trooped in and motioned her to sit. Jee-yun trembled and submitted the false papers, but they ignored her documents and stared rudely across the table. Her gaze faltered.

"How far is your village from the nearest town?" one man barked out. The interpreter translated.

She quickly made up an answer. "Three miles."

The next official asked, "Who occupies the house east of yours? What is the surname and how many are they?"

Jee-yun swiftly invented a name and number.

Before she could take a breath, the third man asked, "How many stairs lead to the ancestral hall? Are they stone or wood?"

All day the officials shot questions at her and carefully recorded her answers.

"What are the market days in town?"

"How many steps is it from your front door to the village entrance?"

"In what directions are there hills? How many hills can be seen from the village entrance?"

"How many tombs are on the hill where your grandfather is buried?"

Her throat dried, but the men refused to provide water. She grew faint, but her captors kept the window shut.

When Jee-yun was finally taken to her cell, she could hardly breathe. The officials had posed several hundred questions and she had fabricated answers to all of them. Their scheme was clear. In a few days, they would repeat their questions. It would be impossible for her to recall all her false replies. Then they would know she wasn't Yung Gim-lan and had no right to enter.

She realized she had fallen into a well-crafted trap. From the barred window, she saw a forest park by the ocean. Her cell contained no chairs or desk, and certainly no paper or pen. But to soothe her nerves, she composed a poem in her head, and then cut the words into the wall with her jade pendant.

Walls of stone and steel rise to surround me,
Windows frame a forest green, ringed by sea.
But I will ride the ocean waves crashing high,
And carry deep desires to meet the sky.

Each day she wrote lines of poetry. It helped the hours creep along. When the officials dragged her back to the interrogation room, she tried to recall her answers but soon confessed she wasn't Yung Gim-lan.

"Who sent you this birth certificate?" demanded her jailers.

She refused to reply. They waited to see who might visit her but Wah-lung suspected a trap and dared not approach. Each day he trudged home from work by himself, hoping a miracle would bring her to his room.

Jee-yun carved more poems onto the wall, but their tone grew grimmer and the images darker.

Why does a heart beat when no one can hear?
How many sorrows can a solitary heart bear?
The wisdom of the past slips with autumn leaves,
Sweep them away, and scatter the seeds.

When she saw horse-drawn carriages trot gaily along the seawall, tears poured from her eyes. When children ran by with colorful kites aloft in the sky, she gripped the iron bars until her hands ached.

The officials grew worried. Some days she refused to eat. Often she spat in their faces; other times she lay on her cot and wouldn't budge.

As she grew thinner and weaker, the officials summoned a Chinatown doctor. Jee-yun shook her head and wouldn't let him touch her. He coaxed her with kind words to try to learn her real identity, but she turned away and wouldn't meet his eyes. When the doctor noticed her wall poems, he copied them down in his notepad. Later, he showed them to the editor of one of Chinatown's newspapers, who praised them and quickly published them.

Soon all Chinatown was marveling at the talented poet imprisoned in Pig Pen. When Wah-lung read the poems, he detected the growing despair and realized he had to act soon. But Pig Pen was tightly guarded.

One warm night, he waited in the shadows of a nearby alley. When the truck came to haul away kitchen waste, he jumped onto the vehicle's back and crouched among the greasy barrels. He held his breath until the sentries at Pig Pen's gate waved the truck through. Then he hopped off and slipped into the building. Approaching footsteps sent him running into a dark corner. But he didn't realize the truck's garbage smells were clinging to him, and the guards easily sniffed him out. He tried to run, but the guards cuffed his hands and ankles and called the police.

In the courtyard, Wah-lung looked helplessly up at the rows of stony barred windows and shouted at the top of his lungs, "Jee-yun, are you there? It's me, Wah-lung. I came to see you! Jee-yun, are you there?"

Jee-yun ran to the window only to see him thrown aboard a paddy wagon. She slid to the floor weeping and choking.

From then on, she wrote no more poems. When she gazed at the distant seawall where young couples strolled freely, the pain cut so deeply that she moaned.

In court, an exhausted Wah-lung appeared before a stern-looking judge. The young man hadn't slept, hadn't eaten and was crushed by his failure to free Jee-yun. When he was pronounced guilty, the judge ordered him deported to China immediately.

"No!" cried Wah-lung. "Let me stay in prison here. My beloved is locked in Pig Pen."

But the judge ignored his plea, because a steamer ticket cost less than a term in prison.

In Pig Pen, Jee-yun wept into her cot until her eyes were swollen and red. Finally, she begged to be sent home. Weary officials issued a deportation order and put her on a freighter bound for Hong Kong.

Imagine the joy when Jee-yun and Wah-lung found each other aboard the ship. They embraced and vowed never to be parted. As the ship left the harbor, they clung to each other and watched Pig Pen and the park's great sea-wall glide by.

But before they got far, a violent storm battered the ship. The cargo of steel beams in the hold shifted and the boat overturned. There were no survivors.

No one in Jee-yun or Wah-lung's family even suspected they had died. Their bodies were lost to flesh-eating fish and corrosive saltwater. The only evidence of their love had been etched into the walls of Pig Pen, and it was there that their two souls returned until the building was torn down.

If you spot Jee-yun and Wah-lung on the seawall one evening, don't be afraid of the young lovers. They are neither angry nor vengeful, for they are content to be in one another's company, and the view of ocean, trees and mountains remains magnificent.

SIX

THE PEDDLER

⊙

THE residents of Chinatown didn't know much about Little Lo, but they all agreed he should never have come to North America. These were not cruel comments, for people genuinely worried about simpletons trying to survive in a harsh new country. Little Lo had no steady job. Instead, he loitered at the game-halls sweeping floors and washing teacups, emptying spittoons and scrubbing brown-stained toilets. No one asked him to do the work, so no one paid him.

But everyone told tales about him.

"I saw him squatting at the back door with a bowl of rice heaped with meat and vegetables. A stray dog ambled by, and Little Lo fed it with his own chopsticks. No wonder he's so thin."

"He was strolling along Main Street with his fly wide open. Passersby were pointing and chuckling, but he paid no attention. When someone finally told him, he bowed at everyone, grinning like some grand entertainer."

"You know he's awkward, right? One day he tripped and fell and thumped down two long flights of stairs. Any normal human would have broken a bone or bruised himself. Instead, he started giggling. The man is crazy!"

Nobody knew Little Lo's exact age because his head was cleanly shaved (to avoid fleas, people muttered). Nor did anyone know his home village because he rarely spoke. Little Lo had no friends, no home other than the gambling tables he slept under, and no known relatives. It was rumored his family in China had sent him abroad to eliminate an embarrassing problem. Others claimed he had been a smart young man until white boys rammed his head against a telephone pole during a robbery.

One day, Old Poon the vegetable peddler won the biggest jackpot ever at fan-tan. He had bet all his savings against the highest odds, and when his number lucked in, he jumped to his feet and bellowed with joy. As the dealer grimly paid out the winnings, Old Poon yelled to the kitchen, "Cook a feast for everyone here! And everyone working tonight gets a big tip!"

But when the old-timer came to Little Lo, his eyes narrowed and he threw an arm over the young man's shoulders.

"I've been worrying about you," he said. "Listen, this is no life, hanging around a gambling parlor. Tell you what. This win lets me return to China, so I'll give you my horse and wagon, and you can take my route. Try and make a living as a peddler."

"A...a h-h-horse of my own?" cried Little Lo. Old Poon nodded.

"A...b-b-business for m-m-me to run?"

"Yes."

Little Lo nodded eagerly, but onlookers shook their heads.

"That idiot can't run a business," they muttered. "The horse will sicken and starve because the fool can't even care for himself."

Old Poon led the way to midtown, where Chinese farmers cultivated acres of land and peddlers slept in crude sheds by the stables. Each morning, they awoke to the impatient grunt of hogs, fresh dew on potent fertilizers and the cluck of anxious chickens. Then they hurried off to work. In the days before electric refrigerators, housewives throughout the city relied on door-to-door peddlers selling fish and eggs, vegetables and fruit. The lady of the house chose whatever was fresh, came at a good price or tickled her fancy that morning. She never had to put on her shoes to go shopping.

Old Poon took Little Lo for a ride to see the route. The wagon rumbled through quiet residential streets lined with green lawns, colorful flowerbeds and shady trees. The houses featured wide doors, generous porches and shiny windows.

Suddenly the hooting and yelling of children shattered the quiet afternoon. Little Lo looked down and saw a crowd of neighborhood youngsters dancing around them, loudly chanting a rhyme. He didn't need to understand the words to feel the sting of insults.

Old Poon drove on without flinching. "Are you afraid?" he asked.

Little Lo shuddered but bravely insisted, "Children will grow up."

They stopped to give the horse some water, and Old Poon said, "Listen, this is a straightforward job, but you have to use your head."

Little Lo giggled.

The older man continued, "Keep your eyes alert, or people will cheat you."

His companion nodded, but Old Poon doubted his advice was sinking in. He rubbed the animal's nose and said, "Horses start their lives wild and cannot be ridden or driven by humans. But once trained, they are transformed into loyal helpers. If a beast can change, so can you."

Little Lo stroked the horse's muzzle and felt warmth spread through his entire body.

All Chinatown watched his first week. To everyone's surprise, he caused no accidents and earned enough to cover his costs. The cynics shrugged.

"That's because Old Poon's horse knows the route by heart and stops at all the correct corners without being told. The idiot can't last. He has no brains."

But Little Lo seemed to have a knack for business. Each evening when the peddlers purchased fresh produce from farmers, they had to hope that their selection would sell the next day. Little Lo seemed to know when housewives wanted radishes for salads instead of cabbage for coleslaw, or when they were short of potatoes and needed great sackfuls for mashing. More often than not, his wagon clattered back to the farm empty. The peddlers also discovered that Little Lo didn't carry pencil and paper. Instead, he kept accounts in his head and always knew which house owed him how much.

"It's lucky the fool finally found a calling," they commented. "Otherwise, he would have starved to death in his old age."

Then Little Lo ran into Tommy, a boy with hair the

color of oranges. The peddler was carrying two heavy baskets to the door when a sudden force exploded beside him and sent him sprawling into the ground. His potatoes and onions rolled in all directions, and the ripe tomatoes were smashed and ruined. When he sat up, a boy was swinging from a rope in the trees that lined the path.

On his next visit, he tripped over a thin wire Tommy had tightened across the path. As Little Lo struggled to his feet, the neighborhood children sprang from hiding places in the bushes, laughing and hooting. He recognized the faces, for just yesterday he had handed them toffee wrapped in colored foil.

When he returned to his wagon, the horse rubbed its nose comfortingly against his chest.

One day, Tommy demanded to know the horse's name.

"An-n-nimals d-d-on't have names," Little Lo replied. He let the boy sit atop the wagon, banging his feet against the seat boards and shouting "Giddy-up!" while he jiggled the reins.

Then Tommy's mother ran out into the street shaking her fist at the peddler. Her face flushed red with anger as she pulled the boy off the wagon and shouted at him, "Do you know how dirty that wagon is? You could catch a disease and die!"

The boy retorted, "But, Mother, you buy his vegetables."

"And I scrub them clean, rinse them four times and boil them thoroughly."

After that, Tommy's pranks resumed. He scattered marbles on the walk to make Little Lo slip, he kicked a soccer ball into the peddler's face, and he planted wads of chewing gum on the doorstep where Little Lo stood to conduct his business.

Each night back at the farm, the weary peddlers boiled rice and ate together. After a long day on the road, they shared their stories.

"She asks for lettuce, so I run to the wagon and bring some. Then she insists on cabbage, and laughs that I can't tell the difference between the two!"

"She promised to pay today, but when I knocked, the house was an empty box. The entire family had packed and moved. She owed me for five weeks of vegetables!"

Little Lo swallowed his rice and didn't say much. He never complained about Tommy. Instead, he tended his horse. Old Poon hadn't taken the best care of it, but Little Lo fed it softened oats, spread ointment over insect bites and provided new shoes, and gradually the horse regained its strength. On hot summer days, it always stopped under shady trees, refusing to budge until Little Lo had sipped cold tea from his jug. On rainy days, it moved faster, as if trying to finish the route quickly. In the fall, when anxious housewives wanted their root cellars filled with beets, carrots and cabbage, the horse pulled extra loads without complaint.

Every night, Little Lo scrubbed his horse with a brush and pulled burrs from its mane and tail. He inspected its teeth and checked its hooves and iron shoes.

"You treat his feet better than your own stinking shoes!" the other peddlers laughed.

As time passed, people in Chinatown heard how Little Lo was now making a living. He installed rubber tires on his wagon for better traction on rain-slicked roads. He helped the other peddlers with sick or injured horses. They heard he wore a raincoat and rubber boots on rainy days, and hummed opera tunes as he drove. People wondered when he might take a trip back to China to show his family the successes he had achieved. But nobody heard about his troubles with Tommy.

One summer Tommy developed a fascination with fire. He squatted by piles of burning branches, blowing on them to make the flames and smoke billow. He shot flaming arrows at a bull's-eye in the middle of the lawn, and charged wildly about without a shirt while brandishing a torch like an ancient warrior.

One day Little Lo saw Tommy dancing around a pile of twigs and branches that he had lit.

"Look at me!" he shouted. "I can walk on fire!"

At the door, his mother greeted Little Lo. He wondered if she ever worried about Tommy playing with fire, but she seemed pleased that he was playing outside and not disturbing her.

"What's nice today?" she asked.

"All n-n-nice," he replied. He showed her cabbage and carrots, tomatoes and potatoes, green beans and peas.

"You have any spinach?" She always asked for whatever he didn't have.

"N-n-no, s-s-spinach all finished."

"How about lettuce?"

"No, none t-t-today. Maybe t-t-tomorrow?"

Suddenly Little Lo heard a screeching as shrill as a whistle. He paused. It was his horse. Then came loud crashing and splintering.

He rushed off. His animal lay half on the road, half on

the neighbor's lawn, surrounded by black smoke, its legs kicking. Flames licked at its back and sides. A bitter smell rose up. The wagon had tipped, spilling everything and oozing blood from flattened tomatoes. Little Lo smelled gasoline. Someone had poured it over the horse and lit a match.

He used his shirt to beat the flames, but couldn't get close because of the horse's panicked kicking. The neighbors came running as the horse made half-weeping, half-bleating sounds. Little Lo ran around the flames and smoke, wailing and moaning. In the background, he heard Tommy whimpering, "It was an accident! I didn't mean to do it! Honest!"

Finally, several women hurried out with pails of water and doused the flames. But it was too late for the horse. It lay panting for breath. Wide strips of flesh were charred, and the glossy big eyes were dulled.

A man came out with a rifle.

"Quick, put it out of misery."

Little Lo shook his head, but the man persisted. Little Lo had never held a gun before, let alone fired one. But somehow he stilled his shaking hands, aimed the barrel and pulled the trigger. The noise of the shot startled him, and the rifle flew from his grip.

The crowd pushed the stiffening horse onto the wagon and set the vehicle upright. Little Lo draped the straps over his shoulders and pulled it back home to the farm. He could not bear the thought of insects devouring the animal's flesh, so he assembled heavy logs and the other peddlers dragged the horse on top of it. Then he set the pyre on fire and let the flames reduce his old friend to ashes.

He went back to that street only once, with another peddler who spoke better English. They confronted Tommy's mother at the front door and demanded financial compensation. She snorted and slammed the door in their faces.

After that, Little Lo never returned again. No one on that street knew he died shortly afterwards, alone in the farm shed. A different man brought fresh vegetables around to sell, but he drove a truck fashioned from an old Model T Ford.

Soon after, Tommy's family moved away and put up a For Sale sign. But the property never sold. Prospective buyers being shown through the house saw a thin bald man leading a horse through the rooms, right through solid walls. Real-estate agents pretended not to notice, but they, too, saw the phantoms clearly and were horrified. The horse's hooves made no sound on the hardwood floors, but bits of mud and dung were always left behind.

Eventually, Tommy's parents stopped paying taxes on the property and let the city seize it. The house was torn down and the lot was reshaped into a park with a sandbox and swings for children.

But nobody plays there at night, not even on hot summer evenings when the park is lit and children run around sweaty and restless. And on Halloween, nobody ever goes trick-or-treating on that street, even though the houses set out pumpkins with deep orange faces lit by candles.

SEVEN

THE BROTHERS

◉

IN China there once lived a poor widow who had two young sons but neither land nor family to support her. Though frail in health, she solicited odd jobs from neighbors, crouched in their paddy fields during planting and harvesting, and sewed late into the night. And she relied on the kindness of clan members and fellow villagers. Without them, she would have had to beg for food and coins from strangers in the market town. She tried to raise honest boys, but villagers told tales about the younger son, Ping, that made her sigh with sorrow.

They said whenever Ping was given a dish of food to take home, he gulped down the choice pieces before his mother and brother ever saw the meal. When he ran small errands for neighbors, he kept the change by claiming the cash had been lost.

When market stall-keepers accused him of stealing, his mother beat him with bamboo, but he grit his teeth and showed no remorse. Within days, she would hear fresh reports of thefts.

Whenever Ping landed in trouble, his mother scolded the older brother.

"Where were you, you stupid thing?"

"Why weren't you watching him?"

"Can't you keep him out of trouble?"

Shek was two years older and always volunteered to do chores for the neighbors in return for a few coins. But the villagers told him, "You're a good boy, but you should learn to talk fast like your brother. Sometimes he's naughty, but he's always quick and clever. He can sweet-talk his way out of any hole."

Shek tried to follow Ping everywhere. He couldn't stop all the mischief because his younger brother always managed to evade him. One day, he saw Ping topple the bamboo scaffolding as workers constructed a towering arch, causing one man to fall and break his leg. But he told no one, not wanting to bring more grief to his mother.

The two boys grew up. But young men who could neither read nor write had no future. They searched nearby towns and ports for work but returned home dusty and penniless. Finally, their mother decided to send them to Gold Mountain, desperately borrowing from money lenders and kinsmen to pay the passage.

At departure time, she reached out and seized Ping. "I can't teach you about honesty any more," she cried. "In the New World, you will have to follow the laws of the land. When you return to the village, come back as a good man. In the meantime, send money so I can hold my head high."

Ping shrugged her off. He wasn't pleased about leaving home and fending for himself. His mother had always washed his clothes and put food on the table.

Then she gave Shek a single piece of advice. "Watch over your brother. It's your duty."

When they arrived in the New World, the brothers split up. Shek joined a salmon-canning crew up north while Ping washed restaurant dishes in the city. Then Shek yanked planks off the chain at a sawmill in the coastal forests while Ping butchered hogs in the interior. Ping enjoyed the freedom of being away from his brother, but his slack work habits often got him fired from jobs, and then he would have to ask Shek to send him money.

Finally, the two ended up together in the city, where Shek borrowed money to buy a farm by the river. The farmhouse was built of logs held in place by plaster and mud, but the soil was dark, soft and fragrant. Shek joyfully flung handfuls of dirt into the air.

"I own land!" he exulted. "I own something that lasts forever." He said to his brother, "Come work with me. Everyone has to buy food, because everyone has to eat. We'll grow rich together."

Ping shook his head. He sneered at the lopsided barn, beat-up truck and battered equipment his brother now owned. The rusty tin roof sagged and leaked, and there was no running water in the house.

"This place stinks of mud and dung," he cried. "I didn't come to Gold Mountain to roll in the dirt like a hog."

He fled downtown and found a job in a laundry. There, great iron boilers roared to heat water and dry the wash. As he stirred sheets and shirts in vats of detergent, he would sweat all day even when it rained or snowed outside. Whenever his boss went to the front counter to serve customers, Ping sneaked out the back door to smoke cigarettes. When he was in a rush to leave, he would rinse the wash only once instead of twice. If customers complained, he always denied any wrongdoing.

As usual, whenever he had spare cash, he went gambling. He played fan-tan, mah-jongg and dominoes. His friends played for high stakes, and money slipped through his fingers like sand. He never sent a penny home because Shek handled the remittances.

Three or four times a year, Shek visited a Chinatown company and handed over an amount to be forwarded to China. Then he went to a letter-writer to have a message written, telling his mother to go to the company's branch office in the market town to retrieve the money. To relieve her worries, Shek always claimed the funds were from the work efforts of both brothers.

Once, after the police raided a game-hall and arrested thirty gamblers, Ping slept on the concrete floor of the jail for three nights before Shek bailed him out. If Ping was lucky enough to win at the tables, he summoned all his friends to feast on bird's nest soup, shark's fin and abalone. Song-girls entertained them, guests danced to the gramophone, and the banquet lasted all night. But he never invited Shek, who frowned on such carefree spending.

A few years later, the Great Depression descended. Factories and mills closed, and workers across the continent lost their jobs. Long lines formed at soup kitchens, and homeless men slept in shantytowns under bridges. Many Chinese booked passage back to the homeland.

When Ping's laundry went bankrupt, he had no choice but to go and live with Shek, who was glad to get a helper and have his brother nearby.

Ping soon discovered the rigors of farm work. When

he met his buddies in Chinatown, he complained at length.

"I start at daybreak, work until dark, swallow some rice, and then sleep a few hours until it's barely bright enough to see my hands in front of me. Chores are always waiting. A second seeding has to go in, seedlings need to be transplanted, or crops must be harvested before insects eat everything. I can never scrub myself clean, my fingernails are permanently black, and my back aches all the time. I am nothing but food for mosquitoes to feast on."

He hated the farm a hundred times more than the laundry. The outhouse was a long walk away, and when it rained, his bed became soggy. He looked for ways out, but Shek did not pay him wages, so there was no opportunity to win at gambling or to buy a train ticket out of town.

So he decided the only way to get money was by improving the farm's income. He challenged the way his brother grew many different vegetables. Shek had reasoned that if carrots didn't sell, then the lettuce would. And if the radish crop turned brown and mushy, then tomatoes would reduce the loss.

Ping noticed that potatoes always sold well, and argued the farm should grow nothing but that one crop.

"It's too much work with different vegetables," he insisted. "Too many plantings, too many diseases, too many things to remember and worry about. With potatoes, you plant them and dig them up, bag them, ship them out, and you are all done. And we can get rich, since the whites eat them every day."

Shek's brow furrowed as he thought about the proposition. Every day, Ping would reframe his arguments and add new information.

"Look at Chung Chuck! He grows only potatoes and has built a new farmhouse and owns three trucks. Even white farmers and politicians call him the King of Potatoes."

"Did you hear? The wholesalers raised the prices paid to potato farmers by five cents a sack! It's the third raise this season."

"Have you seen this? The Marketing Board is giving every housewife in town a free cookbook with a hundred recipes for cooking potatoes! Sales of potatoes are sure to go up."

Gradually, Shek gave in to his brother's position, so next spring, they seeded the fields with only potatoes. There was a bit less work that summer, and a good harvest followed. With the extra income, Ping had money to play with, and Shek sent extra funds home and paid down his debt.

Then Ping had another idea. "You should sell the farm! That way, we can both return home and retire in comfort. We won't ever have to work again!"

"No!" cried Shek. "I'll never find a piece of land so fertile and large in China."

Ping knew his brother was right, because the ancient soil back home had supported crops over many hundreds of years. And the families owning tracts of good land would never sell, no matter what amount was offered. But that didn't stop Ping from insisting on leaving.

The following spring, when the tax inspector visited the farm, Shek was gone. Ping said he had left for China to care for their sick mother. As before, he put in a crop of potatoes, and all summer he weeded and hoed and picked hungry bugs off the young plants. Then he visited a real-estate company and announced he wanted to sell the farm.

One hot day, two men drove in: a sales agent and a buyer. They wandered around, kicked the dike to test its strength and inspected the equipment. They complained about rusty hinges and the mucky puddle at the front door of the barn. Then the buyer went to the outhouse.

Suddenly Ping heard the big fellow scream and saw him flee from the outhouse. His hat flew off, but he didn't bother to stop. When his agent came running, he shouted, "Get me out of here!"

A week later, Ping saw the sales agent at the bank. "What happened that day?" he asked.

The agent drew close and lowered his voice. "That buyer said the outhouse was cold, which he found unusual because the sun had been shining all day. He said when he leaned over the hole to look out the window, someone grabbed him from behind and tried to push him down the hole. He shouted and screamed, braced his arms and legs against the walls. It took all his strength to keep from falling into the muck. When the pushing stopped, he turned around. Nobody was there, and the door was latched on the inside!"

Ping shrugged. "I use the outhouse every day, and nothing has ever happened to me."

Unfortunately, word about this strangeness leaked out, and no other buyers came by.

That year, Ping had a bumper crop of potatoes. He was willing to sell them cheaply to wholesalers, but the

Marketing Board ruled that wholesalers could only buy potatoes tagged by the Board and set at a higher price. Moreover, each farmer could only sell a limited amount of potatoes. This benefited white farmers who grew smaller crops.

To Ping, this meant that no matter how many potatoes he grew, he could only sell a small amount. He and the other Chinese farmers rebelled and kept selling large quantities of potatoes at lower prices. Then the police and white farmers blocked the bridges and inspected all the Chinese trucks trying to pass. If the Board hadn't put tags on their sacks of potatoes, they weren't allowed through. Fights broke out every day.

One evening, Ping loaded his truck with potatoes and sprinted for the wholesalers in town. The roads weren't lit and he had left the truck lamps off to avoid detection. He knew the route by heart and thought no one would spot him. But near the bridge, two cars roared out of a hidden curve and forced him off the road. Ping bounced to a stop, and white men rushed out smelling of whiskey and waving flashlights.

They grabbed Ping and threw him to the ground and kicked him. Ping fought back but he was outnumbered. He felt his nose break and his cheekbone crack as he screamed in pain.

Suddenly he heard his truck engine being fired up, and then the vehicle rolled toward him. One of the white men aimed a flashlight at the steering wheel, but no one was there. Everyone jumped back, shouting and cursing.

The truck stopped and a voice shouted in Chinese, "Get in! Hurry!"

Ping clambered on. It wasn't until the truck reached the main road that he saw that Shek was driving.

Ping gasped and his hands started trembling.

"What do you want?" he asked.

Shek braked and said quietly, "Little Brother, I promised our mother that I would watch out for you."

Then he opened the door, hopped out and vanished into the night.

Ping took a deep breath and dropped his head onto the dashboard and wept bitterly. When he recovered, he drove into town without a word. He delivered his shipment of potatoes, took the money to the steamship agent and bought passage on the next ship to China. He landed in Hong Kong and then a ferry slowly took him up the muddy river to his village.

On reaching home, he fell onto his knees before his mother and knocked his head against the floor.

"Mother, I have committed a terrible wrong," he said in a pained voice. "I pushed Shek into the river when it was running high from the winter meltdown. I thought I was smarter than him, but he wouldn't let me sell the land, not even when he was dead. And when angry farmers almost beat me to death, Shek's spirit rescued me in the nick of time. He was a better man than me."

Ping expected his mother to be angry. Instead she leaned back and sighed.

"What good sons I raised," she said. "Shek looked out for his younger brother even in death, and you came back an honest man. Now I can die with a clear conscience."

EIGHT
ALONE NO LONGER

⊙

IN 1914, the Year of the Tiger, a man named Ko made the most difficult decision of his young life. He said farewell to his sweetheart and journeyed alone to Canada. They had loved each other since their village childhoods, and he promised to return and marry her. In the meantime, his pocket held a photograph. It was black and white, but had been tinted to give her pink cheeks and red lips. They had exchanged studio portraits, and he imagined she studied his picture every day, the same way he worshiped hers.

In Canada, he paid the head tax with borrowed funds, approached a Chinatown job broker, and landed in the kitchen of a downtown restaurant. Day after day, he peeled potatoes, carrots and beets. Week after week, his knife reduced bushels of onions and cabbage to thin slices. His hands grew chapped from cold water, but soon he learned to season roasts of meat, make savory gravies and bake lightweight cakes that could be iced and decorated. It took ten years to clear his debts, but Ko thoroughly mastered the Western kitchen.

During this time, Canada changed its laws and banned

Chinese from entering. Chinatown was furious, for no such rules applied to any other immigrants. But men such as Ko who had already paid the head tax could visit China and re-enter Canada if they had the proper documents.

Finally, Ko shopped for thoughtful gifts, packed his bags and sailed home. His parents welcomed him joyfully, as did his sweetheart. Family and friends gathered to celebrate the wedding, for the devotion between Ko and his bride was well known.

After the rounds of festivities, Ko gently explained that Canada would admit him but not her. She was surprised such cruel laws existed to keep families apart and begged him to stay behind. But he argued there was no future for him in China and promised to return as soon as enough money was saved.

But when he went back to the restaurant where he worked, the doors were locked and newspapers covered the windows. Ko looked elsewhere for work, but jobs were scarce. So he took the train east through the mountains and into the prairies, where every small town had a café run by Chinese. He traveled throughout the three inland provinces, but no café owner would hire him.

The prairies loomed like an ocean of land stretching flat to the edges of the earth. Ko felt small and afraid. There were few trees and no mountains to hide behind. From time to time, distant streaks of lightning attacked the ground and cracked the sky with light. Ko wondered who would inform his wife if a flash of electricity from the sky should hit him.

Then he came to a small town with an ice-rink and four churches, several stores and two schools. It also had an empty café with five dusty booths, a counter with nine stools and living quarters for the owner. The business had been dead for a long time. The bank that owned it wanted to recover some of its money, so it set a low price and lent Ko some money. He bought it and then pumped pails of water to scrub the long mirror, the windows and chairs, the range and the oven.

On opening day, the café leaked aromas of hot coffee, fresh-baked bread and sugar-glazed doughnuts onto the street.

At mid-morning, the bell over the door tinkled and in strode the seed-and-feed storekeeper, a man with an ample belly. After coffee and apple pie, he exclaimed, "Welcome to our town! This tastes wonderful!"

"Very ordinary," Ko said modestly. "You like?"

"Of course. People will fill your place in no time. I guarantee it!" Then he leaned close. "Sure hope you'll stay. Other China men tried to run this place, but they claimed it was haunted and quit."

Ko gulped.

"Didn't the bank warn you? Years ago, this café was so busy that the China man hired a farm girl as a waitress. She worked six days a week, from dawn to dusk. Then he sold the business and returned to China. But the girl had secretly fallen in love with him, and in her sadness she doused herself with kerosene and lit a match. You believe in ghosts?"

Ko just shrugged and let the question go unanswered.

That night, he fell into bed after a steady stream of lunch, coffee break and supper customers. At midnight, a loud crash awoke him. In the kitchen, a dinner plate lay broken on the floor. He frowned. He had washed the dishes in a soapy hurry, so maybe the plate hadn't been stacked properly. He swept up the pieces and went to sleep.

The next night, another noise awoke him. In the dining room, a chair had toppled over. Maybe it hadn't been properly balanced when he swung it onto the table to mop the floor. He set it upright and went back to bed.

On the third night, before going to sleep, Ko fried a steak and made toast, coffee and gravy. He set out cutlery and a napkin and placed the food near the stove to keep warm. Then he switched off the lights.

That night, nothing disturbed him.

From then on, Ko put out a meal each evening. It might be a chicken leg or a hamburger, a slice of roast or beef tongue — whatever the daily special was. In the morning, the food would still be sitting there, cold and dry. He shrugged and concluded ghosts did not eat but could enjoy the aromas instead.

Five years went by, and then another five. Ko developed a steady routine. He kneaded dough for bread early in the morning, he chopped a week's supply of wood every Sunday, and he planted a garden of lettuce and tomatoes. In the summer, the oven and stove roasted him; in the winter, he brought in ice from outside and melted it for drinking water. The townspeople were friendly, but no one invited him home, so he sat alone at nights. He longed to return to his wife and China, but his debt to the bank wasn't paid off yet.

When chores were finished, he wrote letters to his wife describing the work of the cafe. He never mentioned leaving out food in order to keep the peace. Their wedding

DEAD MAN'S GOLD

portrait stood close by, and one glance at her face always eased his loneliness. He had always hoped to start a family, but grimly realized that time was hurtling by without any regard for him. In the mirror, his reflection showed many gray hairs.

One night, a weary Ko left the sink cluttered and fell into bed without washing everything. The next morning, he found all the dishes clean and dried.

Another day, he overslept and awoke just in time to open the door to customers. But he found the kitchen fire roaring, coffee brewed, and cookies browning in the oven.

After this, whenever Ko ever felt lonely in the evenings, he sat by the stove beside the dish of food he had put out. A dreamy feeling would overtake him, and sometimes he saw a woman's face smiling at him. Sometimes he caught a whiff of perfume, a fragrance he recognized from the girls who came to his restaurant. The druggist said farmers' daughters used it in the summertime when water shortages limited the number of baths people could take. On nights before he fell asleep, he would hear a woman humming popular songs from the radio.

Then public attitudes toward the Chinese changed, because China fought with the Allies against Japan, and Chinese Canadians enlisted in the Canadian armed forces. Now that Chinese were viewed as fellow Canadians, immigration laws were amended to admit them in small numbers. Ko jumped for joy and immediately sent for his wife. As excited as a new bridegroom, he counted off the days until her arrival.

At the station, she came down the steps of the bus clutching the railing with hands brown and thin from too much sun and not enough food. During the war, no money could get through to the homeland. Her hair was newly curled, and her sandals were too small.

But Ko still saw the woman he had married years ago. He escorted her around the café, the living quarters and his little garden. He showed her how to open the refrigerator, turn on the neon sign and twist the blinds shut. He planned to teach her a new English sentence every day.

That evening, while he watered his yard, the wind hummed through the tomato vines. He heard a murmuring rush of words.

"I'm going, Ko. She's home, so I'm going..."

He stopped leaving food on the stove that night. And nothing ever disturbed the reunited couple.

But the long separation had taken its toll. Ko's wife tried to prepare traditional meals for him, but they lived so far from a Chinatown that she couldn't find ingredients such as water chestnuts and lotus roots. What she served tasted lifeless and dry. She tried to help him in the kitchen, but didn't know the recipes of the café. Sometimes her bread wouldn't rise or her doughnuts fried up as heavy as rocks. The churchwomen invited her to tea, but she drowned under their high voices and gay laughter.

She longed for China. In her village, women gathered at the river to wash clothes, at the stone courtyard to dry the grain, and under the banyan tree to shell peanuts for roasting. They would laugh and chat and challenge each other's stories. If there was a village wedding or birthday, they came together and cooked enough to feed all the families. On special occasions, opera troupes passed through the village and performed on the open-air stage. She and her friends watched the performances all afternoon and well into the night.

But here, when she watched Ko banter with customers, her heart turned to ice at missing his words. When Chinese newspapers arrived, weeks late, she had to wait for Ko to find a free moment to read to her. She tried to learn English, but her tongue stiffened no matter how she tugged and stretched it. And her brain stewed in a lazy fog, unable to recall new words no matter how often she repeated them.

One day, as she took clean glasses into the café, a child dropped a ball. Transfixed, Ko's wife watched it bounce across the floor. Her neighbor's boy in the village had a similar ball. Without thinking, she began singing a lullaby the women once used at bedtime. All the diners looked up, for they had never heard such a tune. She threw her apron over her face and ran from the room.

After that day, she stopped trying to learn English. When Ko reproached her, she snapped, "I'm too stupid for the New World!"

When he bought her a new dress, she moaned, "The clothes here do not fit me properly."

When he gave her jewelry, she complained, "I'm not as pretty as the women here."

She lost her appetite and couldn't sleep. Her hair began to fall out and her teeth loosened and blackened. Ko took her to a doctor, but she grew weaker until she couldn't walk or sit up. When Ko fed her soup, she cursed him for leaving their homeland. Still, every night he slipped into their bed and let his body keep her warm.

Late one night, her eyes filled with tears and she whispered, "You have been a good husband. I should never have come here. I loved you, but you changed more than I could. Please forgive me." Her head rolled to one side and she stopped breathing.

Ko shook her but found no pulse. All night, he sat beside the stiffening body, weeping silently.

"A curse upon this New World!" he thought. "If I could start over, I would have stayed home, close to my woman. Why work so hard if a man can't have a family?" Finally, his weariness overtook him and he fell asleep.

When he awoke, another day's new light was breaking through the window. The aroma of freshly brewed coffee filled the air, as did the murmur and chuckle of conversations. He jumped when he noticed the bed lay empty.

He ran into the café and saw customers seated at the counter with steaming mugs in their hands. His wife glided by with a pot of hot coffee.

"Good morning, husband," she smiled. "You were weary so I let you sleep. Look how sunny it is today."

Ko grabbed her hands and found them warm and soft. He saw a pink face and bright eyes.

"How did this happen?" he stuttered.

His legs felt weak, and he didn't know what to think. She frowned and gave him a puzzled look. He lunged forward and put his head on her chest, and heard a heart beating steadily.

Then he caught a familiar smell — the scent of a perfume that used to drift through the café on lonely nights.

NINE

FIRST WIFE

◉

I N Middle Creek village in South China, whenever
Lew So-ying's little boy Jee-wah asked about his
father, she would set aside her sewing and repeat her
husband's words.

"Your father lives in the biggest city in Gold Mountain,
where towers loom higher than fifteen pagodas stacked
one atop another. People inside do not climb stairs, but
ascend to the top in a flying cage. Your father's office has a
telephone and electricity, glass windows and a huge table.
He owns a business and a building, and he is always meet-
ing people and signing documents."

Jee-wah listened thoughtfully, trying to imagine the
look of flying cages and electricity. And his chest would
puff out proudly.

As So-ying told these tales, even her own eyes misted
with longing. She pictured stone columns guarding a
grand entrance to a mansion, and saw maids serving meat
to her husband Lok-hay at every meal: fresh fish in the
breakfast rice porridge, strips of lean beef with lunchtime
noodles, and juicy chicken at dinner. In the village, So-
ying's family cooked meat once a week and considered

itself lucky. Her husband sent money but she spent it carefully, paying workers who tended the family's fields, minding her parents-in-law and maintaining the ancestral tombs.

Sometimes Jee-wah asked, "Why does Baba have to work in Gold Mountain?"

"Son, your father is earning money to build a new house here. When he has enough cash for land and carpenters and bricklayers, he will return to the village and relax for the rest of his life."

The boy persisted, "Why doesn't Baba sell his building and business now and come home to be with us?"

"Because he has debts to repay. Because he needs enough money to send you to good schools."

"Can we go and live with Baba in Gold Mountain?"

"No," she replied. "It is not allowed. For many years, Chinese have not been welcome there."

News came that the immigration laws had changed. But Lok-hay did not send for them.

Then the Communists seized power throughout China, vowing to take land and property from the rich and give it to the poor. The new government labeled those who used helpers in their fields as greedy landlords. So-ying's friends and neighbors turned against her, accusing her family of owning too much land and whispering she had secretly buried her gold jewelry. Lok-hay feared for So-ying and Jee-wah's lives and paid smugglers to whisk them to Hong Kong. There, tickets were waiting.

So-ying gasped when the airplane roared off the runway and lifted over the rooftops and then the hills of Hong Kong. When she saw the ocean glittering far below, she shut her eyes, afraid of falling from such a height. How could such steel and metal soar like a bird, she wondered. She felt dizzy when the flight ended, but Lok-hay's friends transported her to the train station in a big automobile with springy seats.

The train ride through the mountains and across the prairies took three days, and Jee-wah sat glued to the window, watching towns and trees and power poles pass by. So-ying rejoiced at the quiet time. The thought of being reunited with Lok-hay after thirteen years brought color to her cheeks. They had wed twenty-five years ago when she was sixteen. He had sailed back to China several times to see her, but only one son had survived the years of war and hunger. And Jee-wah had never seen his father.

As the train chugged along, So-ying dreamed of cooking invigorating soups for her husband. She would sew fitted shirts for him and massage his weary neck. Never had she imagined arriving in Gold Mountain and traveling in such splendid comfort. Now she would witness generations reconnected as her son embraced his father. Lok-hay would show him the ways of North America.

She tied her hair with a bright ribbon and practiced smiling in a mirror. Up and down the corridor she hobbled, trying to master high-heeled shoes. If fellow villagers had seen her, they would have fallen down laughing. The other passengers aboard the train smiled, for So-ying's happiness infected everyone.

When the train reached its destination, a conductor helped her down the steps, and through swirling snowflakes she saw Lok-hay in the crowd.

"That's your baba," she whispered to Jee-wah.

Lok-hay's hair had thinned, but his face glowed and his stomach stuck out. The family shook hands and smiled nervously. Mother and son had never seen their breath puff out like fog in the frigid air.

Lok-hay hurried them into a taxicab, and when it came to a faded brick building, he announced, "I live here. This is the hotel I run."

The sign hung lopsided and its paint was peeling and cracking. On the stairs, a woman wearing a tight dress, crimson makeup and strong perfume stumbled by, weak from too much drink. The hallway reeked of bleach and broadcast the rumble of adults quarreling in small rooms. A tiny window at the hall's end and weak lamps emitted dim light, as if secrets needed shade.

Lok-hay opened a door. "This is your room," he announced. It had puffy wallpaper, two beds as limp as hammocks and a washbasin. When So-ying peered into the closet, a mouse scampered out. The toilet and bath were located down the hall.

So-ying gripped her bag tightly. Jee-wah stared at her with narrowed eyes as though she had lied to him all his life. Her gaze fell to the floor. This was not the gracious life she had pictured in her mind.

Had Lok-hay lied to her? she wondered. Or had she let her imagination fly too wildly?

Then her husband said, "Come, there are people to meet."

Behind the hotel office was a cheerful apartment filled with framed pictures and calendars, upholstered chairs and cushions, a radio and a big box television. A Chinese woman stood up smiling, as did two teenaged girls with curled hair.

Lok-hay cleared his throat. "So-ying, this is Lan, my local wife. Lan, this is my First Wife, So-ying, and my son, Jee-wah. So-ying, meet my local daughters."

So-ying turned and ran to her room. For twenty-five years, Lok-hay's letters had declared affection for her. Not once had he mentioned a second wife. Not once had he mentioned having other children. She dropped onto the bed and burst out weeping. The long trip had exhausted her, and very quickly she cried herself to sleep.

Later, when she saw Lok-hay alone, she whispered, "Why did you not tell me about them?"

"There was no need," he replied briskly. "I never thought the Chinese would be allowed to immigrate again. Caught in between, I decided to have one family here, and one in China."

"You should have told me," she protested. "I am your First Wife."

"You still are," he said. "And you are the mother of my son. You have nothing to fear. Are you angry?"

She looked away and stared at the wall. Eventually she said, "I know that life here was difficult. You were lonely and lacked company."

"Lan is kind and gentle," her husband insisted. "She speaks English and helps me run this hotel."

"But you vowed to come back to China and build a big house."

He looked her straight in the eye. "I would have kept my promise. Lan has no desire to go to China. But now the Communists make our return impossible."

In the following days, the daughters fitted the newcomers with galoshes and showed them the sights of the city. In a department store, So-ying tried to pay but fumbled counting the correct bills. As the sale was rung through, she grabbed the purchases before a clerk bagged them, causing the stepdaughters to redden in embarrassment. When they registered Jee-wah for school, So-ying stood silently as the girls chatted with the principal and signed all the documents. The boy watched his half-sisters intently, as if he already knew they would soon teach him all about the New World.

In the hotel, So-ying watched her husband heave heavy coal into boilers that heated the building, soak bedding in cement tubs, and crawl on his knees to wax and polish the long halls. Lan and Lok-hay ran busy through the day, seven days a week. Lan bent over a sewing machine powered by a foot pedal to mend sheets and towels. She dipped pillowcases into starch before ironing them, and explained to So-ying how this extended the life of the cloth. Even during mealtimes, the telephone rang and boarders banged at the counter to borrow keys, pay rent or bemoan the lack of heat. So-ying offered to help, but Lan said respectfully, "You are the First Wife. You don't need to work."

Every night, her son raced to Lan's apartment to watch television. For hours he sprawled before the swirling lights, mesmerized by the jingles, armed cowboys and constant smiles. Sometimes he fell asleep there and didn't return until morning. When So-ying complained, her husband replied, "This way he will learn English faster."

Now and then, she saw Lok-hay press his lips to Lan's mouth. So-ying longed to smile the same way as Lan. Sometimes, Lok-hay or Lan took the children to the movies, but So-ying stayed home, as she knew no English. She hid her hurt inside like a mound of ice that couldn't melt, and sat alone in her room. The faded, yellowing blossoms on the wallpaper brought her no cheer. The sink was rusty, but no matter how she scrubbed, she could not clean it. When she felt the four walls closing in, she ambled along the corridors of each floor by herself.

On one such stroll, she heard an anguished voice call out, "Save me!"

She looked around. Again she heard the call for help, and followed it to a door. She tapped lightly on the frame.

"Are you all right?"

The door swung open. The curtains were drawn shut but a lamp threw a glow over an old man in bed. He had bushy white hair, a face brown and speckled as a potato, and big-boned hands.

"Please," he cried out, "bend my toes toward my shin. Use your strength, for a terrible pain burns down there."

So-ying obeyed, and the man's face gradually relaxed.

"Sit," he commanded, "and keep an old man company. How long since you came here?"

"Too long," she replied bitterly.

"Me, too," he said. "Seventy-five years."

"Twice my age!" exclaimed So-ying. "I have only been here for four months."

The old man's eyes brightened. "Then you have fresh memories of China. Tell me all you remember."

After that, she visited the old man regularly. On each occasion she told him about her village routines: awaking to the rooster's call, munching cold rice at breakfast, wading through the paddy to supervise planting, lugging water home, shouting over the walls at neighbors. She described tiled roofs tinged with green moss, golden fields at harvest time and soft hills that glowed pink at night. She recalled the people of Middle Creek village: Gossip Chen whose tongue had swelled up and prevented her from speaking, Toothpick Jin who married the shortest girl in the district, Four-Eyes Ming who wore sunglasses to hide his one glass eye, and Fatty May who devoured five bowls of plain rice at every meal because she had never eaten enough as a child.

These memories teased smiles onto So-ying's face. But she feared losing this friend to her son and stepdaughters who dominated the dinnertime conversations, so she told no one about him. After each day's story, the man sighed with immense satisfaction, for he longed to see China again. He called her a godsend who brightened an old man's final dark days.

Then one day she arrived and found his room empty. The curtains were open and sunlight poured in. The bed was neatly made with blankets stretched from side to side.

Downstairs in the office, she asked, "What happened to the man in Room 424?"

The knot in Lok-hay's throat bobbed nervously. "Why, the tenant there died four years ago. That room is haunted. Renters run out, screaming that an old man stands there, rocking and shaking the bed. The door has been locked ever since."

"You mean no one lives there?"

"Not for four years."

So-ying shuddered and fell faint. Then she threw her shoulders back and declared, "I'll take that room. Our son will appreciate having a room to himself."

She moved in and waited. But the old man never came back, even though she stayed in all day with the curtains closed and murmured his name. As the bedside clock ticked on, she tried to recall village life, but the memories wouldn't come without an appreciative audience.

One day at dinner, So-ying watched Jee-wah ignore his bowl, half full of rice. Lok-hay said rice was cheap here and wouldn't force the boy to swallow every grain. His girls ate dainty amounts of rice and preferred raw vegetables. So-ying could barely eat as they munched uncooked spinach and lettuce like water buffalo chewing straw.

Then Jee-wah spoke. "Baba, parents are invited to school to meet the teacher. Will you come?"

So-ying perked up. Here was a chance for Lok-hay and her to go out alone with their son. Here was an opportunity for outsiders to acknowledge she was Jee-wah's mother.

Lok-hay nodded absently. "Of course I will."

Then Jee-wah turned to So-ying. "Ma, I want Lan-Mother to come with Baba. You don't understand English, so what's the use?"

All eyes around the table landed on her. Her heart pounded, and warmth drained out of her body. She stared at the tablecloth and muttered, "Well, if that would be better, then I will stay home."

No one said a word, no one disagreed with her. Afterwards, tears washed her cheeks as she climbed the stairs to her room.

Opening the door, she was startled to find her friend the old man there. Her mind was a muddle as he called out with warmth and concern, "Little Sister, why so sad?"

"I no longer have a son. I am no longer a mother."

The old man drew close. "Want to come with me?"

"No!" She backed off. "I won't die yet!"

"Don't be silly. Who's talking about death?" His voice was calm. "There is a third place for people like us, people trapped by space and time, by events bigger than us. In the third place, our memories become real worlds, and there we live happily until it is time to die. You gave me back my memories of China so I could go there. Will you come, too?"

She did not know what to say.

He asked bluntly, "Tell me, are you happy here?"

Her reply was bitter. "Happy? Can anyone count on joy so far from home?"

The next morning, when So-ying did not show for breakfast, Lok-hay went to look for her. Room 424 was empty. The family searched the entire hotel and the neighborhood before calling the police. They never found her.

But friends of Lok-hay who worked on the trains reported catching glimpses of her riding the train, sitting beside the long windows and watching the scenery fly by. It was the last place where she had been happy.

TEN

REUNITED

◉

IN 1955, when a father he had never met summoned
Tong Lung to North America, the teenager stayed in
bed in Hong Kong for days, playing sick. His father
had worked abroad for many decades in order to send
money home. To maximize these remittances, Ba chose
not to travel across the Pacific for visits, and so Tong grew
up seeing only photographs of his father.

Tong spent Ba's money freely. In Hong Kong there were
Hollywood movies, Top Ten songs from England and the
latest motorbikes. When he and his buddies entered a
restaurant or shop, waiters and clerks bowed and fawned,
knowing that the sons of Gold Mountain men tipped well.
And pretty girls flocked to Tong's good looks and his taste
in Western restaurants, Taiwanese singers and European
fashions.

Then Ba insisted he relocate, and threatened to with-
hold funds if he did not. It was time the boy shouldered
adult responsibilities, he said.

But Tong relished the freedom to spend and party as he
pleased. When one school proved too rigorous, he trans-
ferred to another. Lately, his mother had been preoccupied

with her ailing parents, refugees from China with no other kin. She decided to stay and care for them. Tong suspected his father would prove old-fashioned and strict, for his letters pestered him to do well at school and to obey his mother.

At the airport, his mother asked, "Will you see to your father the same way I nurse my parents?"

Tong turned away. Then, much to his own surprise, tears coursed down his face as he said goodbye to his grandparents. They had been his loving guardians when he was little and his mother worked in a factory.

"Try to change your attitude," Grandmother advised. "Respect your father, otherwise his spirit could return and ruin your life."

Tong stiffened. Modern young men didn't believe in ghosts.

He traveled across the Pacific Ocean by himself and spent four days sleeping upright on a train that crossed the continent. When the train reached its destination, Tong wished it would rumble right through and plunge into the Atlantic.

Under the station's high, ornate ceiling, he spotted Ba, looking just as stiff as he did in the faded wedding photos at home. While other greeters kissed and hugged their loved ones, he and his father shook hands like businessmen. The gray-haired man's strong grip surprised Tong.

"I've waited a long time," his father said.

Outside, the teen went toward the taxi stand.

"Where are you going?" his father shouted. "We're walking."

Luggage in hand, they dodged pedestrians and passed

office towers so tall they nudged low clouds. Streetcars rumbled by on steel rails imbedded in roads jammed with fat grumbling trucks. Hong Kong had big buildings and streetcars, too, but Tong stared at the cars crowding the corners and streaming through the streets. There were more here, and they were bigger, in all colors and with many teenagers in the driver's seats.

As they passed a sugary-smelling coffee shop, Tong offered, "Ba, let me buy you something to drink."

The older man shook his head. "There's tea at home."

They passed a restaurant leaking savory aromas under a marquee of winking lights.

"Are you hungry, Ba? Let me buy you a steak."

His father walked faster. "Do you realize you are spending *my* money?

Finally they reached a street of identical apartment blocks and few trees and stopped at a storefront with a hand-stenciled sign and withered plants in the window.

"This is my laundry," Ba said. "This is where I live."

In the back, bunk beds were propped in a corner of the drying room by a potbellied stove. A refrigerator and stove stood by tubs used for soaking dirty clothes, while a wringer and steam boiler clattered and groaned. The workroom was cramped and hot and had no windows. Fresh air squeezed through the back door only if a breeze chanced that way.

Tong's chest churned with dismay as he recalled Hong Kong workshops where laborers stripped to the waist to sweat all day long. He never imagined his own father working like them.

That first night, Ba took him to a Chinatown restaurant to meet his friends. Tong ate quietly as the Gold Mountain uncles drank and roared at one another. They spoke country dialects and ignored the boy's half-hearted questions. Out of respect for his father, Tong didn't touch the liquor. But the one other teenager at the table drank freely. Ba introduced them and asked Kam to register Tong for school.

Tong hated high school. He flailed in conversations, fumbled for words and thought his fellow students mocked his English. Even slim books took forever to read, and the teacher would erase the blackboard before he had a chance to copy down the assignment. After classes, he was ordered home to iron underwear, feed bedsheets into the mangle, or wrap clean laundry with brown paper. Ba nagged him to practice his English on customers, and often the work lasted until midnight.

Kam smoked cigarettes and bantered with chums and teachers. His father owned several restaurants and lived in a house with a circular driveway. Tong followed his new friend whenever he escaped the laundry.

When Kam suggested Tong buy new clothes, Ba pointed to the garments abandoned by customers. "Find something from there." When Kam invited Tong to Montreal, Ba said, "I've lived here forty years and never gone. Why should you?"

Kam tried to cheer up Tong. He taught him to drive, so they skipped classes and drove down country roads playing the radio. Some nights, they parked in midtown to gaze at the colored lights glowing downtown.

Only when the car was shooting along highways did Tong smile. Only then did he sense freedom and future possibilities. But Kam soon found a steady girlfriend, and Tong resented how the two lovebirds held hands and cooed to each other.

One day after school, Tong passed a car dealership and saw the season's new models. He lingered for a long time, looking at the shiny chrome and colors.

When he reached home, he helped his father fold sheets and said, "Let's buy a car."

"We don't need one."

"We can use it to deliver laundry."

"Our customers pick up."

"Instead of walking downtown to shop, we can drive and save time."

His father exploded. "Why buy a car? To show off? To get the attention of pretty girls? Workers like me don't have automobiles and we don't waste good money. Aren't the streetcars good enough? Besides, where would we get the money?"

Tong shot back, "You have lots saved."

His father glared. "How would you know?"

"I saw your bank book."

The old man drew a furious breath and barked, "That's retirement money! You think I plan to work like this all my life?"

"No!" replied Tong. "You should enjoy life now. With a car, you can go for drives in the countryside or visit friends."

Ba waved him off and started humming his usual opera tunes.

The next day, Tong walked onto the lot of the car dealership. He bent over and saw his face reflected in the shiny paint. He opened the door and inhaled the smell of new upholstery. He wriggled behind the steering wheel, adjusted the mirrors and imagined coasting along an endless highway.

A bow-tied salesman leaned in the window. "You know, it only takes a tiny down payment to take this baby home."

"Down payment?"

"You pay two hundred dollars now and pay the rest over the next five years."

Tong shook his head. "I don't have two hundred dollars."

The salesman grinned. "It's not a lot of money. Ask five people for forty dollars and you've got it. Come on, it's a beautiful day outside. Let's take her for a test drive."

Tong glanced at his watch. He should be home working. Ba would be waiting. The later he returned, the angrier the old man would be. But two hours passed before the teenager tore himself away from the car.

"Forty dollars from five people. That's all I need," he kept thinking.

When he reached his street, police cars and an ambulance with flashing lights blocked the store. He rushed through the onlookers. Officers tried to hold him back, but he saw his father lying limp and bloodstained on the floor.

Someone in a uniform explained, "There was a holdup. Witnesses heard gunshots and saw a masked man run out."

Tong sank to the ground, and his head dropped onto his arms and knees. If he had been home as scheduled, his father might still be alive. Maybe Ba had thought he was at the door when it had been a stranger brandishing a pistol. His father should have handed over the money without fighting back. The cashbox lay ripped and empty. At day's end, it usually brimmed with bills and silver.

Tong shut his eyes and thought how Ba's life resembled the flimsy cashbox. The old man had saved every penny and nickel he could, seeking a peaceful retirement, but now it was too late.

That night, Tong could not sleep as he recalled his grandmother's words. He had not respected his father as she had instructed. In life, Ba had proved so cranky and bitter that it was hard to believe such toughness and strength could suddenly vanish. His father's spirit would be powerful in death.

But the more Tong thought, the angrier he felt. His father had wasted his life. The old man had worked far too hard and never experienced a moment of joy. If he had relaxed about money, they could have eaten well and enjoyed themselves. Instead of fighting, they might have become friends.

He resolved not to repeat his father's mistake.

At the funeral, Ba's friends sat with heads bowed in quiet rows. Tong saw their shabby suits and wrinkled ties and wished he had offered to clean them before the service.

Later, one Gold Mountain uncle approached him and said, "That is a nice photo of your father. I wasn't sure you knew to place a picture at the front to help people remember him."

Another uncle came and said, "Thank you for

announcing cash donations to the clubs your father joined. He subscribed to many good causes."

Someone asked, "Where will lunch be served?"

Tong replied, "In Chinatown's biggest restaurant. I have ordered all his favorite foods."

The Gold Mountain uncles donned their hats and hurried off. Some hadn't eaten breakfast so that they could take advantage of the feast.

A week later, the will was read and Tong received much of his father's money. Right away he purchased the car he had been eyeing and parked it in front of the laundry where everyone could see. Steel and glass and chrome had been shaped into generous curves, and the line of glowing lights above the rear bumper resembled a neon sign. The dashboard lit up like the cockpit of an airplane, with gauges and switches pushing back the dark.

He invited Kam for a drive. The motor accelerated smoothly, and the brand-new smells left them feeling carefree and invincible. They lowered the windows and let the wind clutch their hair. Tong changed lanes recklessly and darted ahead of lumbering trucks.

Suddenly his friend held up a hand. "You hear something?"

"What?"

"Listen hard. Can't you hear?"

Tong shook his head, puzzled.

"Someone is humming Chinese opera." They flicked off the radio and then the humming became distinct. "It's coming from the back seat."

They both recognized Tong's father's voice and his favorite opera tune.

Kam mopped his brow. "You have a ghost in this car."

They sped back to town and Kam leapt out even before the car stopped completely.

When Tong pulled into traffic, the opera tune resumed. He checked his rear-view mirror but saw nothing. The humming persisted and grew louder. Finally, he turned, and there sat his father, wearing the suit he had been buried in.

Tong waited for a crashing blow to his head, for eternal darkness to overwhelm him, for a heavy truck to smash into his windshield. He expected his father to roar out in fury, but nothing happened.

After a while, the old man sighed deeply and said, "Son, you were right. I should have lived a fuller life when I had the chance."

They passed glowing signs and window displays on streets that were clogged with citizens dressed in their best and eager for nightlife.

"It's not too late, Ba," Tong said. "This car belongs to you. You can go wherever it goes. We will drive to Montreal to see Mount Royal, to New York to climb the Statue of Liberty, and to the Atlantic coast to smell the sea salt. I'll take you places so you can see the world and inhale a million new smells."

When he looked behind him, the old man had vanished.

From then on, Tong always left a cushion in the back seat for his father. No matter where the car went, whether through blizzards or ice storms or heat waves, he always felt protected. The car never broke down and never had an accident. And years later, when he chose a bride, had children and purchased a station wagon for his growing family, he made sure his father's cushion went into the new car.

NOTE TO THE READER

After the publication of *Tales from Gold Mountain* in 1989, I found I had more New World folk tales to tell, and they have emerged in this collection as ghost stories, a popular narrative form in China. As with the first collection, I wanted to dramatize the history of the Chinese in North America and create a New World mythology where immigrant stories can be told and retold.

Although I invented all these stories, they are tales much like the ones early Chinese immigrants told one another in bachelor halls or shared with their children and grandchildren during family banquets. Those tales described the very real occupations and immigration laws that the early Chinese experienced when they first came to North America. They also contained suspense and surprise, as well as elements of heartfelt folk culture that would remind Chinese Americans and Chinese Canadians of their ancestors.